THE AWAKENING OF JIM BISHOP

this

changes

things

BEN SHARPTON

Black Rose Writing | Texas

ISBN: 978-1-68433-863-4
PUBLISHED BY BLACK ROSE WRITING
www.blackrosewriting.com

Printed in the United States of America
Suggested Retail Price (SRP) $18.95

The Awakening of Jim Bishop is printed in Baskerville

*As a planet-friendly publisher, Black Rose Writing does its best to eliminate unnecessary waste to reduce paper usage and energy costs, while never compromising the reading experience. As a result, the final word count vs. page count may not meet common expectations.

Cover design by Katherine Sharpton

To the volunteers who selflessly donate energy, resources, sweat, time and love to help those who have nowhere to go when night comes—in particular, the "Room In The Inn" team at Myers Park United Methodist Church in Charlotte, NC. and the leaders of The Haywood Street Congregation and Central United Methodist Church, Asheville, NC.

AUTHOR'S NOTE

The Awakening of Jim Bishop: This Changes Things is a work of fiction. The characters and organizations located in and around Charlotte are fictitious and are not depictions of actual people or institutions. Wesley Memorial Hospital was conceived to further the story. Unfortunately, there is no such hospital in Charlotte. The town of Fair Hope, as well as the description of how it got its name, is also fictitious — the product of the author's intense effort and wild imagination.

ACKNOWLEDGEMENTS

I am grateful to the faculty, staff and students at Queens University who provided support, guidance, and a lot of patience as I wrote *The Awakening of Jim Bishop: This Changes Things*, especially Fred Leebron, Susan Perabo, Naeem Murr and Dan Mueller.

I appreciate the staff of Black Rose Writing for welcoming, publishing and promoting *The Awakening of Jim Bishop: This Changes Things*.

Thank you, Kay, for patiently allowing me the time and support to write this one.

THE AWAKENING OF JIM BISHOP

this
changes
things

CHAPTER ONE

Racing through wet streets in the waning hours of the day, Jim Bishop charged toward uptown Charlotte. His sizable Escalade scissored through traffic, intimidating other drivers — zagging left and right and threatening to crush compact cars in its path. His ringing phone was the checkered flag that started his onslaught of the Friday five o'clock traffic.

The rest had come as a blur. A hospital representative... Jim's wife, Jean... fell into a coma in uptown Charlotte... at Wesley Memorial Hospital... He feared the worst — a long, debilitating coma, unbearable loneliness, emptiness.

On the way, he dialed his brother David, who lived in California, to give him the bad news. His brother took the call without emotion, as if on a heavy sedative.

"David Bishop."

"David, this is Jim. Bad news. Jean's in the hospital. Some kind of a stroke."

"What do the doctors say?"

"I'm on my way there, now. I don't think it's gonna be good."

"Let me know if she gets worse."

David had always been a little off, with fewer social skills than a porcupine. But he was Jim's brother and was the only family Jim had left... besides Jean. He shook off the thought and barreled down the street toward the hospital. A quick query at the front desk, a long ride up the elevator, counting the floor numbers as they digitally appeared in the display box one by one, and Jim found Jean's room.

He was holding her hand when the doctor entered. He said some vagrants had called 911 after she collapsed on the sidewalk. A CT scan revealed a hemorrhagic stroke, brought on by a congenital disorder in the brain called an Arteriovenous Malformation. No one knew she had suffered from the condition, and the disorder was a ticking time bomb. The doctor reassured him that Jean had not been accosted — even her purse had been undisturbed. The homeless people had waited with her until the ambulance arrived, then they disappeared.

Standing beside his wife's bed in the nondescript, antiseptic room, Jim felt detached from the outside world. A window on one brick wall looked out on the streetlight-illuminated parking lot six long stories below. The deadly silence made things seem surreal. During what should be the most intimate time for a family, when warmth and compassion should have filled the room, he faced a chamber of clean, cold emptiness. Once his source for warmth, Jean was now reduced to a soulless body, her mind probably gone forever.

A sterile, plastic tube snaked across the thin blue gown covering her shoulder, stopping just beneath her nostrils and streaming fresh oxygen. Suspended above the bed on a stainless-steel pole, a plastic IV container drip-dripped clear liquid into another tube that drooped down to a needle in Jean's right hand. It had been placed there when she entered the hospital.

A nurse — she said her name was Angela — was working in ER when Jean arrived. She slipped in to check on him during her breaks. Jim could tell she was doing her best to comfort him, but it had little effect. He just felt... numb.

He had known death, but not often. His parents died within a year of each other, back in the late eighties, leaving him and his brother alone. He was in his mid-thirties and their funerals were solemn events without emotion. Various aunts, uncles and cousins passed away over the years and he skipped most of their funerals. He hadn't known them well, and just didn't want to go. When Bob Henshaw, his best friend, best man, and work buddy gave up the ghost fighting the evil cancer demon, his life was celebrated in a massive cathedral full of fellow employees, loved ones, and relatives. Bob's wife asked Jim to speak, but he declined. He would have lost it and the embarrassment would have been too much.

He felt a little sadder with each death. He missed them. Especially Bob.

But he would not miss any of them nearly as much as he would miss Jean.

He held her hand and watched her breath come in quick gasps and felt his own breath mimicking hers — gasp, gasp, gasp. Then the final one, followed by a long sigh, and she was gone. Someone slipped into the room and detached the tubes and wires from the lifeless body and turned off the machines around her. No one attempted to resuscitate her. Years before Jean had made her wish for no extraordinary measures known when she and Jim had prepared their wills. Jim knew the EEGs showed no brain activity, but he still wished he could take back the page, take back the signature, that led to this moment so they could be together just a little longer.

"Why did this happen to us?" He wanted her to sit up and say it would be all right. He longed to hear her reassuring voice, as he had heard it when they learned he couldn't give her children, when she said she forgave him for his failures even though he knew she didn't want to, when he left his job, or his job left him, just a couple of years before.

The empty dusk outside almost swallowed him whole. Jean had always been there for him, but now she was gone and she would never return. Tears tumbled down his face, like the rivulets of water that slid down the windows of his father's car when they drove in the rain during family vacations. He turned to leave the room, stopped halfway to the door and returned to the bed. Raising his face, he stared out the window at nothing but gloomy sky and then back to his wife's lovely, but empty, face.

He had never felt this way before. He was supposed to be the strong one... the decision maker. He drove his fingernails into the palm of his hand to tell himself he was still there, he was still alive. But the pain said nothing about what would come next.

About a half hour later, Nurse Angela came back in. "It's okay to let go now, Jim," she whispered as if the sterile hospital room was an ornate chapel or a crowded library. He followed her lead and stepped back as she slipped the bed sheet over the body's head — a symbolic gesture of closure. The sheet at the end of the bed rose up too high, revealing her left foot. Jim slipped it back down again.

Then, in a soft whisper, Angela said, "Let's go to the lobby, Jim."

His head filled with more questions. *Why Jean? Why not someone else? Why not me? Is this some sort of punishment from a vengeful god for my failures? Am I responsible?* He inhaled a breath of hospital air, sanitized to the point of distraction, and released it and a bit of the sorrow within.

Jim found a generic hospital chair, hard and clinical, built to be as uncomfortable and unwelcoming as possible, in the hallway near the lobby. The short walk had worn him thin. Angela left in silence after touching his shoulder lightly.

Though he didn't want to, Jim willed himself back to the present. He was sitting in a hospital waiting room and he couldn't stay there forever. Placing his hands on the arms of his chair, he tried to push himself up into a standing position, but eased back down, exhausted. The hospital buzzed with activity. Several strangers, testifying concern with worried looks, huddled in small groups around the tiny lobby. A sedated patient rolled by on a gurney. A sleeping old man slumped down so far in his chair he might slide out. Jim wondered how anyone could sleep through the noise of harried voices in odd concert with the excited rant of a sportscaster on a nearby television. Around the corner, someone wailed incessantly. He wondered why no one offered to help the poor lady. This is a hospital, for Pete's sake. Someone should do something.

Jim tried again, and then rose from his vinyl covered chair, left the small lobby, and lumbered down a shiny, nondescript hallway, adorned only by the fuzzy reflections from ceiling lights on the gleaming floor.

Jean would have helped. She always helped.

Room 435. Just a room number, not a name. Like a waiting list number in a bakery or a Social Security number when you needed to complete some stupid form. He urged the door open and slipped inside.

An older woman occupied the first bed in the double room. The second contained another elderly woman. "Can't you get her to shut up?" she insisted, when he entered the room. "Give her some pills or something. Just get her to shut the hell up."

Jim shuffled to the foot of the bed to stand before the wailing woman. She resembled his grandmother when she was on her deathbed in a little hospital in Fayetteville a long, long time ago. Picking up a clipboard attached to the bed, he knew he did not know what the check boxes or scribbles meant, but he recognized a line for the patient's name. She was

Eleanor Brower. "Hello, Mrs. Brower," he said, gazing down upon the blemished and aging face of the frail woman. She clutched her bed sheet against her chin with both hands, as if she was trying to shield her infirm body. Jim fought the urge to hold her.

"Help me, doctor. Help me," she cried. "Will you help me?"

"I'll do what I can," Jim said.

"Help her shut up," the lady in the second bed said, frumping her gray curls

"I haven't seen anyone in days," Eleanor said.

"The other doctor was in here just twenty minutes ago," the second lady countered. "Stood right where you're standing."

"Tell me what's bothering you," Jim said, surprised by his question, but even more surprised that he had asked it. He had no idea of what he was doing or how he could possibly help this poor old lady. Not only was he out of his league, he wasn't even in the sport. Marketing, not medicine, had been his career choice.

Eleanor seemed surprised. She paused a moment but didn't take her eyes from his face. "I'm hurtin'. I need some medicine." She seemed less anxious.

Jim checked out the chart again, as if he knew what he was doing. "This indicates you're getting all of your meds on schedule."

"But I need more. I do."

"I'm sorry, but if you take more, you might get loopy... like me," he said with raised eyebrows.

"Loopy's a hell-ova lot better than wailing," the other lady said.

He hesitated. Then glanced at a photo in a small frame on the table by her bed. "Why don't you tell me about your family?" Jean would have asked that.

"My family?" she asked. "Oh. I love my grandchildren. Amy is in college, in New York or Boston or someplace up north. And Michael's in the Marines. He's so handsome in his uniform," she said, taking a shallow breath between "uni" and "form". She added, "Their mother is a teacher."

"She is not. She's a teacher's aid," second bed said.

Eleanor wrinkled her brow. "She is, too. She'll tell you when she comes to town."

The other patient rolled her eyes. "She lives here and visits her every day."

5

"She does not. She hasn't been here in over a year."

Second bed just huffed and shook her head, as if they'd had this same argument before, perhaps several times.

"I'll bet she comes to visit you this afternoon," Jim said.

"Oh," she said. "Is she in town?"

He nodded.

"It will be so nice to see her."

"I'm sure she is looking forward to seeing you, too." His exhaustion threatened to return, but at least Eleanor had stopped crying.

"I should brush my hair," she said, tugging on the tubes attached to her arms, trying to get out of bed.

"Oh, that's not necessary," Jim said, holding both hands up to stop her. He moved to stand by her. "She said you don't need to do anything. She just wants to see you."

Eleanor settled back, the frown on her forehead softening a bit. She rested her head on the somewhat-flat pillow and breathed in deeply. Jim remained beside her bed and stared into her eyes as she stared back into his. Both remained silent for a while.

In a few moments, after she had slipped into sleep, Jim turned, flashed a faint smile at the woman in the second bed, and left Room 435.

· · ·

In the bustle of the hospital hallway, the man wearing the gleaming white tab of a clerical collar and a deep black shirt, almost bumped into the slow-moving hulk of a man walking toward him. The two stopped in the middle of the hallway like two gunslingers waiting for the other to draw.

Rev. Allen Rhodes didn't like to show impatience. It wasn't... righteous. But his visitation list seemed to be growing by the hour, the traffic was slower than Christmas Eve on a Saturday, and the hospital seemed more crowded than ever.

He realized he had seen him before. He couldn't recall his name — maybe he had visited the church. Maybe... It'd come to him later.

A foot resting on a platform and braced with stainless steel pins stopped his forward motion as a volunteer pushed a wheelchair between the two men through a crossing hallway. The minister had leapt to his right to avoid a painful collision.

Eleanor Brower was in Room 435. She'd been placed there after complaining about everything from stomach pains to migraine headaches. Hospitals didn't like to keep patients as long as Eleanor had been there, but she kept coming up with reasons to run tests, and tests paid the bills.

He knocked lightly and waited to hear a frail voice invite him in. He heard nothing so he knocked again. Opening the door a crack, he peeked into the room. The rather boisterous old lady who occupied the second bed in the room was sitting up, holding a single finger before pursed lips. "Shhhhh. Don't wake her," she whispered. "She hasn't been this quiet in days." When she didn't have anything to complain about, she complained about not having anything to complain about. Wiping his palm across his lips to hide his smile, he slipped into the room and stood for a moment beside Eleanor's bed. After a brief, silent prayer, he left his business card on the bedside table and whispered to the woman in the other bed, "I'll be praying for you, too."

"Pray she'll keep quiet," the lady muttered, staring at the ceiling.

The minister turned and tiptoed back into the hallway.

• • •

A polite volunteer greeted Jim at the Information Desk. Her red hair was streaked with soft streams of gray and her smile was warm.

"Taxi," he muttered. "Would you please call for a taxi?" He would come back for his Escalade later.

"Yes, sir. Would you like Yellow Cab, City Cab, Airport..."

"Any," he said. "Yellow."

She offered a broad, gleaming simper, which was not very reassuring, picked up the phone, and dialed the numbers.

The taxi took much longer than Jim would have preferred but in his state, instantly would've been too long. He felt constricted and constrained and had to get away. His head fell back to the headrest, he breathed the address, and the taxi meandered through city streets toward home.

After the nonstop bustle of the hospital, the house seemed barren, more empty than usual. He looked around at the furniture and trappings. Bookcases, lamps, sofas — unimportant, full of unimportant stuff.

Sinking into the sofa, he resumed the same pose he had in the cab — sagging, with his head against the back, staring at the ceiling. Life would be different now. Nothing would be the same. He had sensed this earlier, and now the reality of it came rushing back.

A knock on the door surprised him, but he remained where he was, head resting on the back of the sofa. The knocking continued. *It might be someone important.* But he closed his exhausted eyes, resolved the visitor would have to call back.

The impatient knock sounded again.

Jim went to the door expecting a nosey neighbor, yanked it open, and was surprised to greet a man wearing a dark shirt and clerical collar. The guy looked familiar.

"Jim?" the minister asked, extending his hand. "I'm Reverend Allen Rhodes. Jean was a member of our church. May I come in?"

Jim couldn't think of a reason or a way to refuse, so he invited the minister into the kitchen where the two men could talk. After declining a drink of water or coffee, the minister said, "I wanted to take a moment of your time to let you know how sorry we are for your loss."

Sorry for your loss sounded as hollow and empty as a rotted-out oak tree. It was polite and objective when the suffering needed more subjective empathy. Jim assumed people used it because they had no idea of what else to say. Allen seemed to recognize that and smiled, showing sympathy, tinged with something else — *exhaustion?* As if realizing how shallow his words seemed, he added, "We will really miss Jean. She was very active at our church and in our community."

"Thank you," Jim said, wondering if that was the right response.

"Is there anything we can do for you?"

Through his exhaustion, he studied the minister. His skin seemed pale — the curse of living in North Carolina in the winter. The wrinkles bordering bloodshot eyes were more pronounced than they should have been for such a young man. Something about him, the way he sat squared off like a boxer, made him seem gritty and tough — not the stereotypical image of a preacher. Jean had liked him, as she had attested several Sundays over lunch, after she came home from church and after he'd slept in late.

Allen said, "Tell me something, a story, about Jean."

"I don't know where to start."

"Anything. A fond memory," Allen said.

Leaning forward on his elbows, Jim said, "Well, Jean loved children. We never had any. I couldn't..." A distant memory of a conference in a medical office with an insensitive physician describing how his sperm appeared so abnormal. Dr. Douche had actually snickered.

Allen didn't respond, but remained seated across the table, hands folded together, eyes following Jim's.

"She used to walk a lot... usually to the park. She told me how she liked to sit on a bench by a pond watching children playing." His chest tightened. His throat constricted. Tears, so unusual for Jim, filled his eyes. He was tired. Allen reached across the table and placed a strong hand on Jim's wrist — calming, reassuring.

With a deep breath, he smiled, "We met as freshmen in college. I majored in business with a minor in marketing and she majored in environmental science. We married after graduation. God, I was so nervous. I threw up twice before the wedding, and I tried to keep her from knowing, but my best man spilled the beans when he toasted us at the reception." He stifled a laugh.

His words came rapidly, propelled from a source inside that had been quiet all day. "She put up with so much from me... Sometimes I lost my temper, but she always calmed me down," Jim said, staring at the table before him. He raised his head, pleased with an old memory. "A few years ago, our neighbor had these two big Labrador Retrievers. I made her laugh when I called them Labrador Relievers because they constantly used our back yard as an above-ground septic tank." He searched the minister's eyes to check to see if he was offended by the off-color statement. Allen was smiling.

"I complained to the owner and got nothing. He told me to go screw... My threats were ignored, and I got mad. I knew Jean wouldn't approve if I punched the guy out, so I came up with another way... I grabbed a pair of dishwashing gloves and a box of large plastic bags out of our kitchen cabinet and culled through every inch of the backyard, carefully scooping up all the Labs had left behind. God, it was rank. Then I dumped the bag of crap on the neighbor's front porch. Two weeks later, he installed a privacy fence and I started calling the dogs Retrievers again. I know, it's silly."

Allen chuckled.

"We were married for more than forty years. She never got mad at me, even when I..." The light above the table glimmered in his eyes. "She was always there for me."

The two men talked about Jean for what seemed like a few more minutes, but when Jim raised his eyes to the clock on the wall, more than an hour had passed. He pushed his chair back from the table. "You must have more important things to do. I should let you get back to work... or home."

Allen followed. "It's all right. This is important."

"No, I'm okay. Really."

"Well, if there is any way I can help, please call me." He placed his business card on the kitchen table.

Jim stared at the card. This visit seemed surreal. The card was a physical reminder that it had really happened.

With that, Rev. Rhodes offered a simple prayer followed by a firm handshake, and he was out the door.

The house was quiet again.

Jim took the business card and placed it under a magnet on the refrigerator and stumbled to his easy chair in the living room. He breathed a deep breath before the tears rushed out again. Sobbing like an infant, moaning, and then crying, and then wailing. All afternoon he had avoided, no prevented, emotions and pain from enveloping him. He'd had to remain strong for her. He couldn't let his feelings show. He couldn't grieve.

His fingers scratched at the arm of the La-Z-Boy. The heel on his left foot bounced like a jackhammer. He stood and wandered into the kitchen, thinking he should eat, but found nothing that interested him. He moved to the sink. Beyond the window, the backyard was lit by a full moon. He poured water into a glass from the faucet, took a sip, and left it on the counter. Walking toward the back of the house, he considered lying down to rest, but when he reached the bedroom doorway, he took one look at the bed she had made up shortly before the attack and then turned back to the living room.

Moonlight from the kitchen window receded with time, making the house seem colder. Darkness soaked up the furniture and the fixtures until the room became only shadows.

Across town, the cyclist prepped for his nightly bike ride. He was a bicycle enthusiast's enthusiast. He was in one local and three online cycle clubs, subscribed to two print versions of cycling magazines, owned four bicycles, and rode in almost every bike road race in the Southeast. Flying down Brevard Street at about ten thirty at night, he knew he was going just a bit too fast, but he loved the thrill of bolting down the road, especially late at night when the traffic was light, the wind roared through his helmet, and the darkness offered a hint of mystery. Late night cycling got his blood pumping and adrenaline flowing. It was his aphrodisiac.

He had all the right gear — a Trek Emonda ALR, which he had picked up just a month earlier at his favorite bike shop, Pearl Izumi shorts and jersey, and Giro Savant MIP's helmet. No one would mistake him for a rookie.

The road on this particular evening was not for rookie riders. For some reason there were more cars than usual. This wasn't a big concern, as long as the road-ragers stayed in their lane and didn't ride his ass. The asphalt was also damp from an evening shower. Some would find a slick road a threat. To him, it was a welcome challenge.

He shouldn't have tried to make the light. It was far enough ahead that he could have successfully rolled to a stop, lifted his shoes from the clips, and lighted onto the damp street surface. But he was feeling good, and often when skillful people feel good, they overreach.

He thought the intersection was empty when he barreled through it, pumping for all his might. He felt the spray flying up from his front wheel soaking the inside of his Izumi's and breathed in the cool evening breeze.

He never saw the BMW.

It broadsided his bike, throwing the cyclist and his bike over the roof of the vehicle and to the middle of the road. A broken rib had pierced his heart and his head had slammed against the hood of the car with such force even Savant headgear couldn't prevent an injury. He was dead before he hit the ground. Given the altitude of his plummet, it's surprising he landed close to the pile of crumpled carbon, steel and Kevlar that once was his proud performance bike. Had he survived, he may have wondered why the taillights on the dark lavender coupe brightened briefly and why the vehicle then sped away into the darkness without stopping.

But the next vehicle did stop... after plowing into the mass of bicycle remains in the road. Screeching to a halt, the paunchy driver, a blond shock of hair falling into his eyes, got out of the late model Corolla and hurried to the lifeless body.

• • •

Kerry Noland, CEO of Bell Intelliservices, sped a little too fast down MLK. Cigarette smoke drifted up from the fingers on her left hand. The roads were empty, so she pushed the BMW harder. It was going to be a busy weekend. Two social events and a late Sunday brunch would tax her tired body, so she had to get home to rest. Then Monday, three meetings with angel investors followed by department head updates and a personal session with her accountant would challenge the normal person, but not Kerry Noland. She had always known she was dif...

The bike was nothing but a speed bump. The stupid cyclist shouldn't have been out so late at night speeding down such a busy street. It was his own fault.

Kerry slammed on the brakes, her car slid to the left and then right and came to a stop a hundred feet away. Her heart rate soared in seconds, and her breath came in short, staccato bursts. She was about to turn around when images from Bell Intelliservices — successful awards, industry accolades, and proud employees — rushed into her mind. She scrutinized the scene through her rearview mirror, checked the side mirrors, and, when she was sure no one had seen the accident, gunned the engine and sped off into the night. Her shoulders shook. She tightened her grip on the steering wheel to steady the car.

The BMW was damaged, no doubt. The bike hit the front fender with such force, there would surely be dents and scrapes. And broken lights. Her image of the road up ahead diminished as the front left headlight dimmed. And, the hood was crunched when the biker smashed into it and flipped over her windshield. She'd have to find some discreet auto bodyshop to repair it as soon as possible. Then, she'd trade the BMW for a new vehicle, maybe a Lexus. A red one.

Kerry Noland sped away toward her uptown apartment.

* * *

Todd Sanders hated his job but it paid the bills while he searched for another. The small staff at Bell was overworked and under-paid, and the bennies were almost nonexistent. The I. T. equipment was sub-par. To top it all off, the CEO, Kerry Noland, was a tyrant, with no understanding of systems and no interest in learning. He avoided her whenever he could, like most employees, but she had a way of sneaking up on employees when they were immersed in their work.

When Noland strutted through the maze of cubicles Todd always found it necessary to go to the print room to change paper, or to the break room to make coffee, or outside to smoke, even though he had never smoked in his life. Noland was known to peer over programmers' shoulders to scrutinize code, which she didn't understand, and to chastise them while doing so. After such visits Todd wondered why she felt she needed to treat coders so badly. She was brutal, bending the programmers to her will much like Sauron in the Lord of the Rings bent the elves to his, turning them into vile orcs. To Noland, employees were less than human.

Todd felt he was wasting his skills at Bell. He would be better suited for Symantec, Oracle, or Apple, but he was stuck here in Charlotte in a low-level telephone customer service company. He'd leave if he could. He just needed a break.

Twenty years ago, about the same time his peers discovered girls, Todd discovered coding. That was his escape. He didn't want to confront the criticism that the jock-holes might throw at him so he would cocoon away in this basement and win level after level of every computer game on the market. He ruled Donkey Kong and Tetris. Call of Duty, Wolfenstein, and Street Fighter bored him. Then, gaming stepped up a notch and he taught himself to write code. "Anyone can use cheats and tips to beat a computer game," he told his next-door neighbor, Jeremy, an equally nerdy, but wired-skinny kid who was also in his middle school biology class. Todd had known Jeremy since elementary school. "Programming. Now, that's fun."

"But that's harder," Jeremy said.

"Harder is better."

He taught himself every language he could, and soon was writing his own versions of games he had already mastered. And, as he created, he became a code warrior. When he graduated from college, it was easy to choose any company he wanted — they all needed competent programmers. Graduate degree? Who cared, as long as he knew C, Java, Ruby on Rails, and later, Objective-C for the mobile industry. He was the lord of his programming domain.

For a while.

These days, software engineers were a dime a dozen. Universities turned them out like the web turned out cryptocurrency. Competition became intense, and those without higher degrees, no matter how adept, were not given a second look. Maybe someday the perfect spot in the perfect company might come along and someone would see what his skillset could bring to their organization. Then, he would be able to bail from Bell.

This latest project — patching their Lubbock software to protect users against Microsoft's screw ups, had drained Todd of any energy he had. He had been yanked off his primary project to improve the on-boarding process for new Bell call centers at the last minute, arguably without cause since upper management had known of this pending software update for over two weeks. But they didn't consider it necessary to let analysts know until the last possible moment and he was the person selected to stay late to fix the problem.

This extra work was ill-timed. He had planned to meet his former fiancé, Mandy, after work. He hadn't seen her in three weeks and had hoped to get back together. She had been reluctant to even meet with Todd, but after a lot of persuasion he'd arranged to drop by her apartment after work. Speeding down the street on this dark and damp night, he realized "after work" was a little later than he had expected. He had intended to pick up flowers, but that was no longer possible. His cell vibrated and he pulled it from his pocket to see she was calling, again, undoubtedly to find out why he'd stood her up.

The car ahead swerved slightly, flashed the brake lights as it came to a stop, then sped off into the darkness. Moments later, Todd's aging Corolla bounded over the hunk of bicycle in the street. He jammed on his brakes and his car careened to the curb like a raft in white water. Slumping back into the driver's seat, he sucked in a deep breath. Tired, overworked, and distracted by the phone call, he paused to reassess his situation — to figure out what had just happened.

He'd run over a bicyclist. He climbed out of his car with some difficulty because the bike handlebars had melded with the undercarriage blocking the driver's door.

Todd ran back to the biker's body, which lay still on the wet asphalt. Kneeling down, he reached for the man's pulse. He didn't think he could feel a heartbeat, but then, he wasn't a medical professional. He wanted to believe the man was still alive but feared the worst.

Somehow he managed to find his cell and dial 911, but the violent shakes continued to wrack his pudgy frame. His voice trembled when he talked with the operator. "I... I think I've killed... I've hit someone on... He was on a bicycle. He was right in front of me and I couldn't..."

"Sir?" the operator said more than asked. "Can you tell me where you are?"

He paused and surveyed the neighborhood around him. "I'm... I'm on the corner of Martin Luther King and Brevard. A restaurant of some sort is back behind me on the corner and a couple of hotels... Oh, God. I couldn't stop."

"Take a deep breath, sir," she responded. "I will dispatch a patrol car to your area immediately. Tell me what happened?"

"You'd better send an ambulance, too. I think this guy's hurt real bad."

"The bicyclist?"

"Yeah. He doesn't seem to be..." With that, he silenced himself. He'd seen enough TV cop shows to know not to admit anything without an attorney, but he'd already screwed up. At that moment he wished he, instead of the cyclist, was lying in the middle of the street.

The wet drizzle picked up again, flattening his hair and dripping down onto his face. It also washed fresh blood from the corpse before him. At first, Todd tried to shield the lifeless face from the rain, fearful that it might somehow wash away important evidence, hindering the pending investigation and his chance to prove his innocence. Realizing his efforts were futile, he sat back in a puddle and let the rain fall, unheeded.

Todd never thought about Mandy.

Angela Griffin rushed through the glass exit doors of Wesley Memorial Hospital to her aging Honda at the far side of the parking lot. She was late. She tended to be late too often, but an influx of meth overdose patients required her last minute assistance, so she'd stayed longer than usual. Her thin, almost fragile frame ached in every joint. Her fourth decade of life was much tougher than earlier ones, so far.

Days like this almost made her forget why she chose nursing as a career. The money was almost okay — it would be nice if she made more, and these days she needed every cent to support herself and her thirteen-year-old daughter. The camaraderie among the nursing staff was a plus, but certainly not sufficient to make her soldier through days like this. Ultimately, she surmised, nursing was worth it because of the patients. They needed help and that added meaning, purpose. Like Jim Bishop. Angela had met Jim earlier that day when his wife was brought through the emergency room after suffering a stroke. When she was transferred to intensive care, Angela checked in on him during her break. You could see the pain in his empty eyes, touched with smoldering anger.

She knew her destiny would be medicine back in high school. Track and field was not a glamorous sport and the student body avoided meets like sinners avoided church, but Donnie Graham was a miler. So, Angela came to enjoy, or appear to enjoy, track meets. She caught Donnie's attention the second week of the season, and, by the third week, they were going steady. Donnie's body was solid, with strong shoulders and thick thighs. In some ways, he was much different than the other milers — thin, long-legged bands of rubber, slinking down the track toward the finish line.

She felt comfortable in Donnie's muscular arms, as safe and secure as a skinny, flat-chested, high school freshman could feel. Mid-season, all that changed.

She was sitting on the front row during the mile run, cheering Donnie as he led the pack on lap three. Then, a rookie freshman from another school tried to make his move around Donnie, but cut in too close. Their legs tangled and they stumbled. Donnie caught his balance and regained his pace, but the freshman fell, catching himself with his left hand. Angela heard his forearm crack from where she sat in the bleachers. She stared as he writhed on the track, holding his arm in pain as the other milers dodged him and moved on. His coach was far away, at the other end of the field, so Angela ran over to the boy without thinking. A white, splintery length of bone jutted from his skin just below his hand. Deep red blood flowed onto the asphalt. Angela knelt beside him and cradled the appendage in her hands. It seemed to help.

Another member from his team — a shot putter, she thought — saw the injury, leaned over, and threw up.

Donnie dashed through the finish line, unaware that the boy had fallen. He searched the stands for Angela without luck. He turned his head to the small crowd that had gathered on the track and his eyes met hers with a look of contempt reserved only for a traitor.

She knew then they would break up.

She also knew she was destined for a position to help others. By the time the coach reached the runner, she had decided to go to nursing school following graduation.

She pushed her green Honda through the interstate traffic, down the ramp to one of the nicer Myers Park neighborhoods, arriving at the Reynold's house at about nine fifteen. Sweeping her hair over her ears to appear a bit more... presentable, she rang the doorbell. Pam Reynolds met her and reassured her that her daughter was fine and comfortable. "Emma and Taylor have been in her room all evening." Then, leaning in and mocking astonishment, "I think they've been texting boys."

"I'm so sorry I took so long. I feel I'm taking advantage..."

"No. Taylor loves having Emma over. They get along so well."

She was sincere, but sincerity didn't pardon the imposition. "Time to go, Emma," she called up the stairs. Pam's house was spotless, even the carpeted stairs. It reminded Angela that women who were married to well-off men had time and energy to take care of their homes — or at least to hire someone to do so.

"In a minute, Mom," floated back down from Taylor's room.

"It's time," Angela called back.

"Another rough day at the hospital?" Pam asked.

"No more than usual," Angela responded, but she hated usual. "We'll have Taylor over next weekend, okay?... Oh, wait. Her father has her then. It's fall softball tournament season. Maybe the next."

Pam smiled and nodded.

After considerable coaxing, they coerced Emma into saying goodbye and joined her mother for the trip home. Clambering down the staircase like a prisoner heading back to jail, she barely looked at Angela. She waved from the passenger window as they backed out of the Reynold's driveway.

Angela focused on the road ahead while her daughter typed and swiped her phone in the seat beside her. Angela wished she would put the damn phone down and talk with her but knew she wouldn't. Emma hadn't said more than twenty words at a time since the divorce. It was worse when she visited her father's for "Dad time", after which she wouldn't talk for a couple of days. Angela couldn't compete with her former husband and the trappings that only someone on a successful dentist's salary could afford.

Up ahead, she saw the remnant of a car accident. A body in the road, a car pulled to the side, and a man sitting on the curb with his head in his hands could only mean one thing. She slowed down. Somewhere behind her she could hear the ambulance siren heading her way.

Emma turned her head just a bit in Angela's direction and toward the accident.

Angela could have pulled over. She should have stopped. Someone needed help. She knew how to help. If she had, it would have signaled an important value lesson to her daughter that we help when we are needed.

But she was exhausted. She had helped people all day, and she needed rest. The ambulance was coming. She probably couldn't do anything, anyway. Emma was tired too and would want to go home.

Her car crept by the accident and she watched the area closely. Fighting the voices arguing in her head, she yielded to the one that said to move on.

. . .

Rev. Allen Rhode's Chevy was over a decade old and had a couple of hundred thousand miles on the odometer to prove it. One day he'd trade it in, but not yet. Funds were tight, it was paid for, and it got him from here to there.

He let his mind wander as he chugged down the road, heading to the church parsonage. It had been a long day — a prayer breakfast, followed by staff meetings, counseling sessions, a hospital visit, and a couple of longer-than-he-wanted committee meetings. He'd missed dinner. Again. He knew Grace would understand, as most ministers' wives understood, but it was wearing him down. He was tired. His fingers had little grip on the steering wheel.

The ambulance shot past him like a tomahawk missile, lights flaring and siren blasting, as it flew up the wet street. Within a few minutes, he caught up to the stopped vehicle, which now was flanked by two police cars. A quick glance told Allen a car had hit a bicyclist. The body was laying in the middle of the lane. A damaged car was pulled to the curb and burning flares seemed to be everywhere.

He slowed to a crawl and slid past the vehicle. It was late. Grace was waiting. He was exhausted, but someone needed help.

Breathing in fresh air through his open window, he turned on his flashers, and came to a stop along the side of MLK. A young man, probably the driver of the damaged Corolla, sat on the curb, head in hands. The police seemed to be wrapping up their report and the EMTs were loading a body into the ambulance. Allen introduced himself to them as a minister and asked if he could help.

"Hi, Father," one said, as he slid the gurney into the back of the truck. "You might wanna talk with the kid over there. He has a mild case of shock, but not enough to take him to the hospital."

A quick look at the body before the body bag was zipped shut, a prayer, and Allen pulled away to talk with the young man on the curb. He sat beside him, elbows resting on his knees.

"You okay?" he asked. The question was only an opener. He could tell the kid was messed up.

A long pause. "Yeah."

"Looks really bad."

"I didn't see him," the words flowed like a gushing river. "I must have been too tired... A lot of time at work. I didn't have anything to drink. I've never done anything like this before. I don't know what's going to happen next. Do you think I'll go to jail? What am I going to tell my friends? Oh, my God."

Allen placed a gentle hand on his soft shoulder, encouraging the kid to talk and trying to calm him down at the same time. "What's your name?"

"Todd. Todd Sanders." He then added, "But you can call me Mud."

An attempt at humor, even self-deprecating, was a good sign. "Todd, I'm Reverend Allen Rhodes."

"I don't know what I'm going to do. I can't go to prison..."

Allen spoke softly. "What did the policeman say?"

"He gave me an alcohol test and then took my information and said they'd call me next week, maybe Monday. He told me to stay in Charlotte 'till then."

"Well, that's a good sign. Since you weren't drinking and don't have a record..." Allen assumed what he had said was true, "you'll probably get charged, but placed on probation."

"Really?"

"Could be. But there may be some sort of fine."

"God, I didn't mean to do it. It just happened. I never saw the guy."

"I know. Things seem really bad right now, but you'll make it through this."

The young man sighed and slumped further.

"You should contact an attorney," Allen added.

The young man nodded.

"I can recommend someone from my church, if you want..."

They sat on the curb together for several more minutes, neither saying a word. A tow truck backed up to Todd's car and prepared to haul it away, Allen asked, "You need a ride home?"

Todd shrugged.

As the truck towed his car down the wet street, Todd gave directions to his apartment in NODA, and Allen drove the young man the short distance. Neither spoke during the ride.

Todd opened the door of the car to exit and Allen placed his hand on the young man's arm. "You will get through this, Todd."

He nodded.

"Here," Allen said, handing over his business card. "Call me if I can do anything... absolutely anything to help."

Todd accepted the card and stuffed it into his pocket without a second glance. He walked trance-like to his apartment door, wounded beyond belief.

Allen waited until he had entered the apartment building before putting his car into gear and slipping away.

. . .

In the dark entryway of a closed store on Brevard Street, something moved. The doorway provided sufficient shelter from the incessant drizzle of rain, a brisk breeze, and prying eyes. It was the perfect hideaway for one who had nowhere else to go. The figure had huddled into the shadows before the accident. From that vantage point, the shiny black car was clearly visible, as was the second incident with the older car.

"Not good. Shouldn't have happened. Not good."

The bright lights of the police car frightened the homeless woman. Regardless of whether she had done anything, the lights warned that someone was in trouble. Often that someone was innocent. And often, she was that someone.

The bright lights of the ambulance saddened Sheryl. Someone was hurt. Someone had died. She wrapped thin arms around the swollen area of her belly as she watched.

After the ambulance left, and the police car left, and the strange man was taken away by another man who had stopped by, the witness huddled back deeper into the doorway and tried to return to sleep.

CHAPTER TWO

At six the next morning, Jim came to the conclusion he was not going to fall asleep, so he arose from his easy chair and went into the kitchen for coffee. The black liquid did little to energize him. He went out front to retrieve the morning paper, remembered he hadn't checked the mail, so he emptied the mailbox of envelopes and fliers and stumbled back inside. Back at the table, he separated the bills from the junk and set each stack aside. Retrieving the paper, he scanned the headlines, but didn't have enough interest or energy to read any further than that.

He poured himself another cup of coffee and sat back in his chair to stare out the window. The flowerbeds were in immaculate shape — Jean loved to plant and prune flowers and bushes of all kinds. The grass needed mowing — his job, but it could wait a few more days until he had more energy. Birds were cleaning out the last remaining birdseed Jean had added to the feeders before she... before the stroke. He made a point to remember to fill them later.

In the master bathroom, he rummaged through the meds in his medicine cabinet, searching for vitamins, assuming they might help in some way through this stressful time. Behind several little round plastic containers of drugs that had outdated expirations, he found them and downed one with water captured by his hand under the faucet. He drove his electric razor across his forest-like stubble and stared at his droopy red-eyed reflection. He turned on the shower, stripped off the clothes he'd worn all night, and stepped under the warming spray. When he finished he felt better—the coffee must have kicked in and his skin no longer felt like the discarded carcass of a dead snake.

He returned to the living room, assumed his place in his easy chair, and surveyed mementoes from life he and Jean had built. Photos in mismatched frames showed the two on ocean cruises, at corporate events, with his brother...

David! He had to give the terrible news to him. They had talked to each other when Jean became sick, and David asked Jim to let him know if she passed away — a crass way of talking about an ill person, but David's way, nonetheless.

David worked every Saturday morning. He didn't have anything else to do. It was about seven-thirty in Sacramento, but David would already be at work at the architectural firm downtown, drawing lines and half circles, moving boxes around on the screen, and printing large copies on the huge copier at one end of the hall. He had worked there for years and the job was a perfect fit, allowing him to spend hours immersed in tiny design details without talking with another soul. Most people would have moved up the ladder as their company grew, but he wasn't manager material. People were too messy for David, unlike the drawings he created in his tiny cube. He was comfortable. He was safe. That's the way he wanted it. Jim dialed his number.

"David Bishop," he said. Short. To the point.

"David, this is your brother, Jim." He had no idea why he introduced himself when he called his brother, but he always did.

"Yes?"

"Jean passed..." Tears came from out of nowhere, surprising Jim and making him angry that he couldn't talk to his own brother without breaking down. "Jean passed away last night," he managed to say, afraid David might come back with, "I knew it." But he didn't.

"Oh."

"I thought you'd want to know."

"Yeah. When's the funeral?" Straight to the point.

"I haven't firmed up the plans yet, but probably Wednesday afternoon."

"Mmmm. I'll probably have to ask for time off."

"I'd appreciate that. Jean would have liked for you to be here with me."

"I'll take the late night flight on Tuesday and be there in the morning. I think it arrives at five forty-five. I'll get a rental."

"It will sure be good to see you, David." He wanted, for once, for his brother to say something like, "Of course, Bro.," or "You bet."

Instead, David said, "Me, too."

"Bye, David."

Calls with his brother never lasted long. If Jim tried to dig deeper, David's phrases would just get more succinct. It was his way. He couldn't help it. Empathy, for him, was impossible.

Then, "Jim..." David said. "I am sorry."

Not much, but he'd take it. "I'll see you Wednesday morning."

Despite his poor communication skills, the call with David did seem to chase away loneliness for a bit. Jim decided against making lunch, opting instead for more solitude, thinking of Jean in his easy chair in the living room.

• • •

Monday morning, based on advice from a friend of a friend with connections, Kerry Noland found herself inside a tiny auto body shop off a side alley in the Third Ward district. Dust caked the surface of everything in the small office and the smell of auto paint was so heavy it was difficult to breathe. The manager, a tall, fifty-something-year-old commoner still sporting acne scars, handed over the estimate. At the bottom the words, "Additional Labor," indicated she would have to pay triple for the work.

"Do you have a loaner?" she asked. It was worth a shot.

The man scoffed. "Unfortunately, all of our courtesy vehicles are out today with other customers."

She left the dusty linoleum tile floor of the office for the uneven bricks in the alley. When she reached South Tryon, she hailed a cab for Bell Intelliservices. The cab approached I-77 and she sat back and practiced her ritual of going over the planned events for the day. But her thoughts were interrupted by a vivid recollection of the accident, or so-called accident. She read the article in the Charlotte Observer on her iPad that detailed how a cyclist had been hit and killed late Friday night in Uptown

Charlotte. The article indicated a man had been charged, his name withheld.

Bell Intelliservices occupied several floors in one of the cities' many skyscrapers. The view of the city was breathtaking. From here, one could see the Bank of America Stadium below and the suburbs in the distance that stretched toward the Blue Ridge beyond. Someone once said if you threw a stone from there you'd either hit another skyscraper of a construction crane erecting one. It reminded Kerry Noland that the future was truly bright for those willing to do anything to pursue it.

She nodded to her office assistant, walked through her office into her private washroom to scrub away the grit from the body shop, and stood before the giant mirror above the gleaming sink fixtures. Glancing at a digital clock shining through the upper right corner of the glass, she reminded herself of her schedule: three more late afternoon meetings followed by dinner with a potential investor who wore her out with his asinine questions. She wouldn't get home until after nine o'clock. *Typical*.

She could use a little help.

Normally, to give her a competitive edge, she'd take a dose of Concerta. During stressful periods, she'd boost her energy and focus with a tab of Ritalin.

Reaching into her purse, she sought a small, ornate pill case, opened the lid and extracted one yellow tablet. Pouring water into a glass from a bottle of *Evian*, she downed the pill followed by a shake of her chin.

The face in the mirror radiated confidence like the elegant chandelier overhead that illuminated the entire room. She was the CEO of this business and the business was a success. Sometimes she had to get mean. If being bitchy was required to push her organization forward, she would bitch better than anyone else. Kerry got things done.

Not like her Dad. He never got anything done. He was a worthless weakling. He...

The countenance in the glass paled and age wrinkled her eyes. Her smile dipped and her shoulders slumped. The image stared back at her, empty. Shaking hands reached for the engineered quartz countertop and moisture dampened the eyes in the reflection. Tears are a sign of weakness so she wiped them away. Eye shadow smudged into the blush on her cheeks. Reaching into her purse, she extracted a tissue and makeup remover and systematically rubbed away the streaked cosmetics until the naked image in the mirror looked little like the high-powered executive of a one-billion-dollar company.

She stared.

When she couldn't stand it any longer, she reapplied fresh makeup. Base, eye makeup and highlighter followed by a power-color lipstick completed her warpaint. A brush-sweep to her hair and she was ready again to face the world.

As her red Christian Louboutins tapped in rhythm down the tile floor, her thoughts returned to the accident, which had floated in her subconscious since Friday just under her regular thoughts, waiting to bubble up to the surface. Her initial reaction to the news report had been relief. They had a suspect and it wasn't her. Now, she wondered who the guy charged with the accident was. Maybe he had been drinking. If so, perhaps Karma had dictated his arrest. Maybe it was an older person, and he wouldn't have long to regret the event. She discounted that thought since no old geezers would be out that late on a rainy Friday night.

No matter how she tried to spin it, she was the one who had killed the cyclist and she would have to live with that for the rest of her life. Such events had a way of ruining a weak person, often in subtle, suppressed ways, but they could make a strong person even stronger. Kerry prided herself in her strength.

She marched back toward her office, leaving most of the stress, the pain, and the memory of her father behind. When she reached the elevator, she made a hasty decision to drop in on the I.T. Department, just to keep them on their toes. After all, I.T. was behind on critical tasks once again. That cost the company money, and that made her look bad to investors.

As the doors opened, employees scattered like roaches when lights clicked on. Kerry smiled. Whenever she made eye contact with any of the remaining programming geeks, that employee would turn away except for a twenty-something who sat up straight and tall in his cubicle. A placard hanging on the side of his cube indicated his name was Steve Thurmond. Kerry had met him before and had nicknamed him, "Suck-up Steve." He had emailed several harebrained proposals for improvement of the department to her. Rumor was he wanted... he lusted after, the I.T. Director's job. Ron Davies was the current director of I.T. He always wore a three-piece suit and cowboy boots — one of his ways to proclaim his separateness from both established and untraditional business people. He looked stupid.

She surveyed all the other cubicles in the large room. In the far corner, the door to the Men's room opened and a slender stick of a man wearing a three-piece suit stepped out. "There you are, Ronnie," Kerry called. At the sound of her voice, he double-timed his pace to meet her in the middle of the room.

"Why is that cubicle empty?" Kerry demanded when he was still twenty feet away.

"Well, that's Todd Sander's cube. He didn't come in today. Somebody said he was in an accident or something."

"But wasn't he working on the on-boarding project? It should have been completed by now," Kerry announced.

Ron could have played an undertaker in a classic horror movie. His face was ashen, his eyes were bloodshot, and deep bags hung below them. "I'll pull a couple of programmers off some other projects — the legacy upgrade — and we'll crank it out."

"And what about the legacy upgrade?" She did nothing to soften her voice.

"We'll put in a couple of late nights and get that done on schedule," he said, his voice still low.

She leaned in. "Your labor costs are already too high. Overtime is killing your department... and our company."

Davies' pale cheeks blotched red. "Yes, ma'am," he mumbled.

With that, she turned on her heels and marched away, satisfied she was in control. Her heels clicked in quick staccato across the lobby as she headed back to the elevator and her office.

"Have a great day, Ms. Noland," Steve Thurmond called as she walked by his cubicle.

Shove it.

That afternoon, it all came rushing back to knock Jim off his feet. Jean's death, the empty house, the restless night — it was all he could take. He paced the room like a hungry tiger in a zoo, surveying everything but seeing nothing. A sofa pillow seemed out of place, so he threw it against the wall. It did nothing to relieve his anger so he grabbed a glass from the kitchen counter and hurled it into the fireplace. Picking up a picture frame, he prepared to heave it after the water glass when he glanced down into Jean's smiling face. He stopped and set it back on the side table with a reverence reserved for the most precious things.

To keep from destroying the entire house, he exploded out the back door into the yard where Jean had placed each plant, each flower, each bush, with the kind of care only an angel could provide. Birds of one kind or another cheeped a melody and the sky was a bright shade of blue. It shouldn't have been so brilliant. It should have been dark gray, overcast and filling with rain clouds. The yard was too beautiful, too perfect for a time of loss.

Jim turned to go back inside. Climbing up two steps, he stopped with his hand on the doorknob. If he went inside, he'd only destroy more of his house. He couldn't stay outside for the same reason. He was lost with nowhere to go. His knees buckled and he descended the steps. He leaned his head to his hands... to support its weight... to hide the tears. Was this how life was going to be without her? How could he survive the dark emptiness? In the back of his mind, the burning question he had from the moment he heard about her stroke. *Why?*

* * *

She'd do anything for Emma. Like most mothers, Angela loved her daughter more than life itself — an easy thing to say, but it was true.

Standing by the front window, she watched Emma's father pull into the driveway. Another Dad's Night. The court had insisted on giving her ex two nights a week after the divorce. During travel ball season she spent most of the time with her father in nearby cities where he coached her girls' fastpitch softball team in organized tournaments. Angela hated those long, dark nights and she hated Evan, her ex-husband.

The car remained in the driveway too long. She wanted to run to the front door and yell at Evan, "Let her go!" But fear that he might retaliate by trying to take custody of her daughter cemented her feet to the floor. Then the passenger door opened and Emma extended one cleated foot followed by the other. Red clay painted one leg — it was obvious she'd seen a lot of play-time, much of it on her rump as she slid into base. She dragged her backpack and bat bag from the car and found her way, stoop-shouldered, up the walk to the front porch. She looked too tired to climb the steps. She hadn't slept last night... again.

Angela stepped up to the front door to help her daughter inside. Emma seemed to ignore her. She dropped her backpack and bat bag to the floor and headed for the back of the house.

"How'd it go?"

Emma shrugged.

"Hey. I was thinking we might go shopping this evening."

"I'm tired. I think I'll just go to my room."

"We can have our nails done."

"They're good," she called from the hallway. Her bedroom door shut.

Angela stared down the now empty hallway with a soreness in her stomach and an empty heart.

. . .

The chapel was half full. A few of Jim's friends from work... former work, mostly subordinates, showed up. Neither Kerry Noland nor any of the C-level executives from Bell were there. A retired couple who lived next door sat nearby. The man prided himself in raising Labrador Retrievers. Most of the visitors were from organizations Jean had joined over the years — book club members, elementary school volunteers, Catawba River activists, and a cooking class. Angela Griffen sat behind Jim.

And David was with him. He stood about the same height as Jim, but David was not slender, not thin. He was flat out skinny. Like Jim, his hairline had receded, but unlike Jim who brushed his hair as he always had, David had his cut so close it was almost bald, as if he was saying, "I'm not losing my hair. I choose to cut it all this short." He would say his opinions were based on principal, but others called him pretty damn dogmatic — the sort of man who, had he been a teacher in a pass/fail class, would have failed students on a subjective essay just for disagreeing with him. Jim had long assumed there was some deficiency

— some hormonal imbalance — that made David's metabolism sky high, his head bald, his tolerance void, and his empathy so, so very low.

But Jim loved him. They were of the same blood. David's presence proved he wanted to care, wanted to support his brother, even if his efforts missed the mark.

Rev. Rhodes led a respectful and somewhat uplifting service with words of comfort and soft music. He recited a couple of the stories about Jean that Jim had told him the night she died. He had asked Jim to speak, but he declined.

The reception was a casual but muted affair, with tons of food and lots of condolences. Jim buried his emotions, put on a sincere smile, and thanked everyone for coming. That was all he could do.

Guests nibbled on tiny ham and cheese sandwiches, fruit, and assorted cold vegetables. In an hour or so the reception wound down as they slipped away. With each exit, Jim's soul grew more empty.

"You gonna be okay?" David asked as the last of the mourners left.

Jim nodded.

"I can stay longer."

"No, that's not necessary, David, but I appreciate the offer." Such empathy was uncharacteristic of his brother, and Jim recognized it took extra effort for David to express it. "Let's grab some dinner before you go to the airport."

CHAPTER THREE

Todd turned to *Living Waters*, a young, energetic body of faithful people who gathered regularly for prayer and worship. In three short years, the church had grown from a tight circle of believers in someone's home to a throng numbering in the low thousands, spurred on by a dynamic young minister and upbeat worship services. Much to Todd's surprise, Steve Thurmond, the co-worker who had always treated him with contempt fit for a reprobate, tossed him a lifeline when he invited him to church.

And church was all he wanted it to be.

When he walked through the tall, glass doors of the new cathedral, he was surprised to be greeted with a warm handshake from Steve. "So glad you could make it, Todd," he announced, pulling their clasped hands closer in, as if dragging him inside. "Meet some of my friends. Mark, Kimberly, Lauren? This is Todd."

Joining the group gathered around a coffee bar that would rival any Starbucks, Todd felt warm — from the coffee in the chilly lobby and the kindness of his new friends. Within seconds he was surrounded by his peers, and some younger than he, asking where he lived, where he worked, what he did in his spare time. Their overwhelming attention would have smothered some, but Todd welcomed it like water to a parched man. *Who'da thought? Water at Living Waters church.*

"What's going on with the court?" Steve asked when they were alone after the service. He hadn't seemed interested in Todd's legal troubles at work.

"My lawyer says the judge is going to give me probation."

"What a relief."

"I'm lucky."

Steve patted his shoulder. "Hey! We're going out for lunch. Wanna join us?"

Applebee's was crowded and noisy, but Todd felt welcomed. "How long have you lived in Charlotte?" "Where'd you go to school?" "Do you play volleyball? We've got a great volleyball league at *Living Waters*." They all seemed so friendly, so kind, and he drank it in. The one who interested him most was Carley, a fragile and demure girl about his own age.

"How long have you been going to *Living Waters*," he asked.

"About ten months... almost a year," she replied. "I moved here from Wisconsin."

"Why'd you move?" he asked, hoping it wasn't with a boyfriend.

"Job. I'm in Human Resources at *Red Ventures*."

"Wow," Todd said. "Good outfit. You guys aren't looking for any coders, are you?"

"All the time," she said.

"Sign me up!"

She gave Todd her email address and cell phone number, told him to send her his CV, and the world became a better place.

Life was pivoting. Life was good.

* * *

On a blustery January morning, Jim wandered into a neighborhood coffee shop just to be near a few other people and ordered a medium-sized coffee — latte, grande, americano, macchiato, whipped and dripped, with a cherry on top? "I don't know, just coffee, I guess." He glanced out the front window to see a disheveled old man shivering beneath the awning. The plate glass was a see-through barrier between the world of poverty and the world of excess, the biting cold and the soothing warmth. He sipped his exorbitant coffee in a safe building surrounded by dozens of well-off, well-dressed men and women, chatting about nothing, enjoying the soft music playing in concealed speakers, and warming their backsides in front of a crackling fire in the shop's fireplace. *Fireplace!* Fifteen steps away, a man leaned into the cold wind, grasping his thin and ragged jacket between his fists, and stepping from left foot to right foot to try to get warm. Left. Right. Left. The March of the Frozen.

Surveying the room, Jim noticed everyone was focused elsewhere — their friends, their electronic devices, themselves. *Inconsiderate, selfish, entitled jerks.* Leaving his coffee on the counter, he walked through the front door without a plan, but propelled by an urge to... do something. No one else seemed concerned. "Hi," he said to the old man. The grizzled guy's ragged beard fluttered in the wind. He nodded. At his feet was a cardboard sign, scribbled with blue ink that said, "Vietnam Vet. Can you help?" Next to it, a paper coffee cup — obviously extracted from one of the nearby trash cans — contained a little change.

"Come inside. Let me buy you a cup of coffee."

The old guy shook his head. "They won't let me in there."

"Huh?"

"They won't let me go in there."

Jim reached out and grasped the guy by his elbow. "They will now," he said and coerced the man, struggling, inside.

The pair stumbled to the counter where Jim ordered a large cup of coffee for his new friend. The barista hesitated, his mouth open to speak, but when Jim stared him down he rang up the order and prepped the coffee.

The old man looked nervous, like a kid dragged into a dentist office. He clasped his hands together as if to avoid touching anything, lest he be reprimanded. The barista kept his eyes on them as they moved away from the counter. A young lady wrinkled her nose and huddled closer to a pod of other young ladies when Jim and the man walked by. The group opened up a bit to let her in — the herd welcoming one of its own. Heads turned and voices whispered. The two men pulled up stools to a high-top in the back where the table should have been hard to notice, but still there were suspicious glances and outright stares. Three men retreated from an adjacent table to one on the opposite side of the restaurant. A guy wearing a tweed jacket peered over the edge of the laptop screen in front of him, but turned away when his eyes caught Jim's. Only one person, thin paperback on the table before her, glanced up and smiled at the two.

Jim leaned over the table, surveyed the man across from him who resembled a skinny Santa Claus, and said, "Are you from around here?"

"I guess I'm from all over." He took a sip from his cup. "Coffee tastes good. Better than shelter coffee."

"Glad you like it."

"'Course, shelter coffee tastes as bad as that crap we had in 'Nam."

"When were you there?"

"Seventy to seventy-two."

"Was it rough?"

"You ain't got no idea. Nobody came back the same."

"Do you have any family in Charlotte?" Jim asked.

"Nah. My wife lives over the border in Filbert."

"That's a hike. So where do you call home? Where did you grow up?"

The old man's eyes faded, then brightened. "Home is where the heart is, right?" He announced. "Hee-hee-hee. Home is where the heart is..." His eyebrows danced.

"How long have you been on the street?"

"You ask a lot of questions," the old guy said. "You ain't a cop, are you?"

Jim chuckled and shook his head. "No. It's nothing like that." He felt his fingers tighten and stifled the need to crack his knuckles. "A couple weeks ago a lady was taking a census of homeless people in uptown Charlotte. She had a stroke. Did you hear anything about that?"

"Don't think I did."

"The woman was my wife."

"Well, I wasn't there. I didn't do nuthin'."

"A couple of people she was talking to tried to help her... They called for an ambulance."

"Anything missin'?"

Jim shook his head. "No. In fact, they were very kind. Jean passed away, and I felt I should... well, I wanted to thank the people who were there to help."

Another sip of coffee and skinny Santa Claus said, "I did hear a couple at the shelter say they were with a lady awhile back when she passed out."

"Shelter?"

"Yeah. Up on Trion. Charlotte Shelter."

"Do you know who?"

"Can't say I do. I just heard the talk," he said. "You might want to talk to the director."

The coffee in Jim's cup was a black hole, sucking his hope away.

The old man leaned in, and in a soft whisper said, "Sorry about your wife... That sorta thing changes you."

Jim nodded, fighting back tears.

The man's dirty fingers rubbed up and down on the table like he might be turning a light switch on and off. He glanced around the room. "These people make me nervous — make me feel alone."

"Nervous?"

"Yeah. They don't think much of me."

"They're not too fond of me, either. I think we're too old for them," Jim said.

The old man cracked a smile, then took a draw on his coffee. "Their loss."

"You know, now that you mention it, I feel alone in here, too. I don't know any of these people," Jim added.

"You don't come here?" Skinny Santa asked.

"Nah. The coffee isn't that great." Jim crumpled his cup and tossed it into the recycle bin. "Swish! That's three points for the Old Farts." Then he turned back to Skinny Santa. "You know, I'm really glad you came inside. It's nice to have someone my age to talk with."

"Well, I didn't have a lot to say about it. You dragged my butt in here."

"Do you have anywhere to go when it's cold like this?"

"I'll try the shelters tonight, but they fill up pretty quick when it's this cold. Sometimes I go to that alley-way behind that fancy French restaurant on South. If I'm lucky, I can find some pretty tasty food in the dumpster back there. Heh, heh."

The idea of dumpster diving made Jim cringe, so he considered offering to put the man up at his house. Would the old man rob him? Make his house stink? Refuse to leave? Maybe he should put him up in a hotel.

"You know why you feel lonely in here?" Skinny Santa said, nodding over his shoulder to the group standing by the fireplace.

Jim shook his head.

"It ain't 'cause you don't know these people." His eyes scanned the coffee shop. "It's cause you ain't known."

Jim turned and eyed the faces that crowded the coffee shop. The old guy was right. No one knew him. He wasn't relevant. Maybe it was his age, or his occupation, or lack of an occupation. He was not important. They couldn't have cared less about him. He was a ghost... that is, until now.

"When people know you, you ain't lonely," the guy said, as if trying to explain his point again. His eyes lit up again. "'To know, know, know me, is to love, love, love me,'" he sang, waving both index fingers back and forth like a conductor leading an orchestra. "The Teddy Bears, 1958. Hee-hee-hee." Eyebrows danced again.

Jim chuckled but tossed a quick glance over his shoulder at the other coffee shop patrons.

The skinny old man stood to go. "Thanks, again, for the Jitter Juice," he said. "I gotta get to the soup kitchen over on Drexel. They run out on cold days."

Jim reached up and grasped his elbow again. "Wait. I'll buy you a sandwich here."

The old guy surveyed the room and shook his head. "Nope. They don't know me here, neither." He headed for the door again.

It occurred to Jim that *he* didn't know the man. Struggling to think of something to say, he called, "Hey. What's your name?"

The old guy's eyes sought Jim's across the room. "Eugene... Call me Gene," he said. He turned and was gone.

Jim stared at the door for a long time.

· · ·

No matter how she tried to shake it, Kerry's thoughts returned to Todd Sanders. The little fat kid in I.T. had taken the fall for her without knowing it. She had read the papers. She knew he had been charged with hitting the cyclist on MLK. She had heard the talk. What were the odds that he would work for her?

And she knew this was best.

On her morning jog around Myers Park, passing one stately brick manor after another, she reminded herself again why it was good that Todd, and not she, had been charged. Her angel investors trusted her to guide her organization to increase ROI and there would be none of that if she left. Without her, potential mergers would vanish, instantly leaving the company to drift and face bankruptcy, proving devastating to over a thousand employees at Bell. Layoffs would be rampant and employees would suffer. In fact, the entire city of Charlotte would suffer.

A cramp attacked her side, and she muscled through it.

But this way, things would be all right. She would survive, as would the investors and the company and the employees.

The painful cramp intensified and she stopped jogging. She leaned forward, left hand on a large oak tree beside the sidewalk and her right on her torso as she forced herself to breathe. In. Out. In.

It was best this way. What else could she do?

Her father, dear old dad, would have caved. He would have turned himself in to the police and possibly faced prison time, unlike Todd, who just got probation and service. Dad would have cried like a baby and once again, Mom would have to work harder to support the family.

The pain subsided and her breathing evened. She started to run again when the stabbing pain came back with fury, as if someone was branding her side with a red-hot poker. Doubling over at the waist and then falling to her knees, she wept. It burned one side of her gut and hung on like a leech.

Her dad. Todd. The pressures at Bell. The pain. For the moment, it was all she could take. She sat on the sidewalk, knees drawn up and elbows hugging them tight. More pain. Straightening out, she lay on her back, placing her hand, again, on her side, as if that might alleviate the pain. It didn't. The sun, distant and faint in the gray, cloudy sky, laughed down at her. The sidewalk beneath her shoulders felt like ice laced with gritty chunks of rock salt. Tears didn't help. They interfered with her breathing and she thought she might pass out. Wouldn't the media love that — *Local CEO Faints On Morning Jog*.

A young, fresh-faced lady stopped pushing her baby carriage long enough to look down on Kerry and ask if she needed help. Kerry brushed her away with a hand wave.

With each move scorching her torso, she placed a hand on the concrete and turned onto her hands and knees, and then mounted one foot followed by the other. She pushed into a squat and into standing. The effort sapped her energy but not her pride. Too exhausted to run, she turned and walked home.

•

Gene's comments stuck in Jim's mind all afternoon. He had left the coffeeshop before lunch. Now he was anxious to find a place where he was known, or could be. And, he hoped to find the nice people who had helped Jean along the way. He'd need a way to verify her helpers, so he scrounged through several photo albums until he came across a recent 5X7 picture of her. He placed it in his vehicle's glovebox.

The temperature was in the forties and dropping and there were people in Charlotte, like Gene, who would be cold, so Jim drove to an army surplus store on Independence Boulevard. Inside camping gear, supplies, military uniforms, emergency rations, and more flanked him on his quest. He found blankets — old rough cotton coverings of various dark colors — as if waiting for him on an old table beneath a hanging light. He stacked up ten and took them to the register. The guy behind the counter looked old enough to have brought everything in the store with him straight from the front lines of World War II. After stuffing his mountain of military bedding in the back seat of his SUV, Jim drove to the First Ward in search of the needy.

He didn't find any.

He felt like he was in an old deserted wild west town. Half-way expecting a couple of tumbleweeds to blow across the road, Jim wondered how the businesses here survived.

Coming to streets and alleys rumored to have higher-than-average crime rates, he thought the destitute might live there. He drove down to Trade Street where the protests over the killing of Lamar Scott had taken place the previous year. Nothing. He parked and looked around inside the Charlotte Mecklenburg Library because he'd heard the homeless went there for warmth and to use their computers for job searches. He stopped by diners and gas stations. *Where is a needy person when you want him?*

Late in the day, when the sun threatened to pull the plug, a patrol car stopped Jim's Escalade.

The cop looked in the backseat and spied the stack of blankets. "So, what brings you uptown, Mister Bishop," the officer asked, handing Jim his license.

"You're not going to believe this..."

"Try me. I've probably heard it before."

Jim studied the officer's face. "Well... You see..."

A loud voice blurted something out of the microphone the police officer had attached to the upper lapel of his uniform. He clicked the button on the mic and mumbled something back.

"I'm looking for some homeless people... No, that's not right." Jim tried again. "A few weeks ago my wife died. She had a stroke while taking a census of the homeless in this neighborhood. Some of the people she was talking to tried to help. They called for an ambulance. They looked out for her. So I want to thank them for helping her. I bought these blankets to give them and to other people who might be able to use them. It's gonna be a cold night." His words sounded like a late night weatherman... a bad one.

The officer studied Jim's eyes, looked into the back seat again at the pile of blankets, looked back at Jim and then into the backseat once more. "You're right," he said. "That's one I haven't heard." Placing his hands on his hips, he surveyed the buildings that lined the street. "Mr. Bishop, I appreciate what you're trying to do, but this part of town is where you don't want to be after dark."

Jim nodded. Looking over the officer's shoulder, about three blocks up Tryon, he saw a frail old lady, pushing a grocery cart loaded with bags and clothes into an alley.

"I recommend you donate them to Goodwill, or Salvation Army, or someplace like that. They have the distribution network and the knowledge of the area to get them into the right hands."

"Thank you, officer," Jim said, still watching the alley.

"I'm serious. You don't want to be here in about an hour."

"Yes, sir."

With that, the officer nodded and returned to his patrol car. Jim watched him say something to his partner, who shook his head, and then the cruiser drove away.

Ignoring the officer's warning, he assumed the old woman with the grocery cart might appreciate a gift, something to help keep her warm, so he removed a couple of blankets and journeyed up the street. When he reached the alley, it was empty. He followed her steps into the dying light when something or someone slammed into his side, knocking the breath from his lungs. The blankets followed him to the hard concrete below. Someone landed a kick to the back of his head, followed by several punches to his face. Jim struggled to fight back, arms flailing without making much contact. Someone else rummaged through his pockets. "Got 'em," he yelled, dragging his cell and his wallet. The three disappeared into the coming darkness.

They were gone in less than three minutes.

Jim rested his pounding head on the nearest blanket. *What the hell?* He placed a finger against his cheek and drew back a bloody finger. His lips were bleeding and his head ached. *How stupid...* Leaning forward, he pulled himself up, retrieved the blankets strewn across the sidewalk, and stumbled back to where he'd left his Escalade. The hubcaps had vanished.

He managed to pull himself into the driver's seat and start the car. Dictating "Wesley Memorial Hospital" into the GPS, he pulled out into the street and arrived at the emergency room within a few minutes. After he stumbled inside, the receptionist checked him in and he was taken to an examination room in the back.

Jim was surprised to see Angela Griffen walk through the doorway.

"Jim!" she exclaimed. "I heard you were here. What happened?"

He shook his head.

"Tell me," she insisted. She took his vital signs as he tried to explain.

"It's really stupid. I'm such an idiot. Since Jean died, I've wanted to thank the people who tried to help her. So, it's a cold night, and I bought some blankets to give to them and to other homeless people. Dumb."

"But a noble effort," Angela said, placing a stethoscope to his arm while taking his blood pressure.

"Well, I couldn't find anyone and I got mugged."

"Looks like they beat you pretty bad. What hurts the most?"

Jim refrained from saying, "Everything." A deep breath and he said, "You mean besides my pride? I banged my head pretty hard on the sidewalk."

"Okay. I'll mention that to the doctor. He'll be here in a moment." She jotted some notes on a computer tablet. "In the meantime, how have you really been? Are you all right?" She leaned against a nearby cabinet, arms crossed. The cross examination zeroed in on his life since Jean.

"I get by. I feel a little lost, but I'm okay." He shrugged. "My cooking sucks."

A knock on the door and the doctor stepped inside. Angela said she'd check on him a little later and stepped back into the hallway.

Devious-looking stainless steel devices covered virtually every spot on the laminate counter tops, which sat below matching laminate cabinets in which more devious devices undoubtedly resided. The tiny room closed in on him. The doctor, rotund and in a white lab coat, who must have neglected every medical recommendation about healthy nutrition, made the room seem even smaller. He wheezed as he breathed.

Jim thought of Jean and wondered how he had gotten into this mess.

. . .

Angela knocked lightly on the door and stepped inside. Jim sat on a plastic chair, looking like a lost puppy — a big lost puppy.

"Well?"

"Just waiting to get the word I can go."

"Let me take a look." She used a sterile pad to wipe away the grime and swabbed his scrapes and cuts with a disinfectant. Then she covered them with light bandages. Standing back she said, "Not bad. I think you'll live."

"As long as I don't pull another stunt like I did tonight," Jim said.

With her hands on her hips, she remembered how broken-hearted he was when his wife died. She could tell there was a lot of goodness inside this man. "Don't give up too soon," she said. "Just figure out how to do it right, okay? You'll get it."

"Can I go home, now?"

"Not, yet. The doctor wants you to wait in the lobby for half an hour, just to make sure you'll be safe to drive."

"I'll be fine."

"Uh, huh."

She escorted him to a chair that faced a television playing a sports highlight program. He eased down into the chair as the talking heads of the sports world made announcements and prognostications over her shoulder. She studied her watch and then placed her hand on his shoulder. "Jim, why don't you let me drive you home?"

"I appreciate that, but it's not necessary." He waved her off.

"That way I'll be sure you get home safely," she added, flashing her warmest smile. "Let me see if I can arrange to leave early." She walked behind the reception desk and keyed something into a terminal.

When she looked up, Jim Bishop was gone.

Weighted down by his loss of Jean and the thumping he'd received from the muggers earlier, Jim pulled out of the hospital parking lot slower than normal. He hurt all over — banged head, bruised side, and empty heart. He just wanted to go home. The sun had set an hour earlier and a bright moon illuminated the buildings on both sides of his SUV. Driving onto I-277, he headed north and realized he had caught the wrong entrance ramp and was now driving in the opposite direction of his home. *Thanks, Charlotte roads.* He took the 12th Street exit and a quick right onto N. Tryon , searching for an empty parking lot where he could turn around.

The lot in front of the Charlotte Homeless Shelter was empty of cars but full of people. A long row of bodies, dark in the shadows of the large, bare building, strung out down the street like a writhing, slowly dying earthworm. The crowd was silent, formed of men and women with garbage bags, tote bags and backpacks, each awaiting their turn. Clouds of condensation rose above each person's head as frigid air met their warm breath.

When he opened his SUV door, a cold wind blasted into the cab. He grabbed a heavy jacket from the back seat, and then as an afterthought, the stack of blankets he'd purchased earlier. Walking alongside the line of homeless, he scanned the faces, not really knowing what he was looking for. He pulled a photo from his shirt pocket and approached a ragged couple huddling together against the cold. The man's thin, gray jacket was torn at the elbow. His scraggly beard pointed at the asphalt. The girl appeared to be somewhat younger. She wore a shirtsleeve blouse and huddled beneath one side of his jacket for warmth. The knees of her jeans had horizontal rips... not fashionable, genuine.

"Any chance you've seen this woman?" Jim asked, holding Jean's photo in the air before their faces. "She does volunteer work around here. She's my wife..."

"Sorry, Man," the guy said. "We just got here from Pittsburg... to get out of the cold." He pulled the girl closer to him. "We ain't seen nobody, except the people here."

Jim moved down the line and held the photo up before a woman wrapped in a blanket, not unlike those Jim carried. She shook her head.

An old man wearing a ski cap over his balding head peered over her shoulder at the picture. "Don't look familiar to me."

"I think I seen her," someone toward the back of the line called.

Jim spun about.

"Hey, I think I saw her earlier today... over by the stadium," and older man, white beard shuddering in the wind. "Is there a reward?"

Shoulders sagging, Jim said, "No. She died a few weeks ago and someone around here helped her. I just wanted to say thanks."

"Yeah," white beard said. "It was last week. She needed change for a parking meter, and I gave her all I had."

Jim felt someone at his elbow. He turned to a short, skinny man huddling beneath a hooded jacket that was heavier, but just as old as the clothes of the people in line. "He doesn't know her," the man said, pulling Jim by the elbow toward the concrete block shelter. "He's just trying to scam you." As he steered Jim toward the entrance, he introduced himself as the center director. "Are those for us?" he asked, eyeing the blankets beneath Jim's arm.

"Oh, yes," he handed the stack to the guy who had pulled his dark blue hood from his head, revealing more facial wrinkles than a man his age should have.

"Thank you," the director said. "These will help a lot." He gave the stack to a woman standing just inside the building with some brief instructions. Then he turned back to Jim. "Would you mind if... Can I see your wife's picture?"

Jim handed it over.

"Oh, yes... Jean, right?" Jim felt an odd sense of hope. "I used to see her uptown from time to time. She usually gave out bottled water to the people she met there. Haven't seen her in a couple months, though." He locked eyes with Jim's as he handed the photo back. "You said she passed?"

Jim nodded.

"I'm so sorry. She was a good woman. Had a good heart."

Jim felt the muscles in his throat tighten. He nodded. "She had a stroke. Someone at the hospital said some homeless people were with her. They called for an ambulance..."

"Most of these folks are like that. A few..." he nodded toward the middle of the line, "Like Vern back there... They're just looking for a handout. But the majority of these people aren't like that."

Jim surveyed the line. "Do you usually have this many people staying here?"

"No, but it's a cold night. They need shelter when the temp drops below freezing, so we pack them in. Sometimes we have more than we can handle."

Jim turned back inside. "Looks like you've got a good operation... a lot of volunteers. Do they come every night?"

"Oh, no. That'd burn them out. Some come once a month. A few, more often."

Jim watched the work going on before him. No one slacked off. Everyone seemed to care.

"Of course," the center director said, "there's always room for one more." He gave Jim a sideways glance, asking a question rather than a statement.

"I'm impressed with what you're doing here," Jim said.

"Why don't you do this," the little guy said. "Hang around for a few more minutes. Chat with some of our guests. Talk to some volunteers. After you get home, if you're interested in learning more, give me a call.

We can make room for you... just like we make room for them." He waved his arm before the crowd of men setting up their sleeping areas for the night.

Jim leaned back against the bare concrete wall as the circus played out before him. Tonight, no one made waves. Everyone settled in for the night. It was cold outside, and the shelter welcomed them.

Leaving the big room where the men stayed, he stepped out into the hallway. A long line of "guests" were awaiting their turn for dinner. A few talked together, some laughed, but most of the people just waited. "Hey! That's the guy who was looking for those people uptown!" a man in the line shouted.

A few people glanced his way. One man's eyes shifted nervously from left to right.

"Hey, you!"

Jim turned.

"Hey, Mister!" the voice said.

The crowd stretched apart like pulled taffy, like Moses' sea, as if the king's army was pushing them away to make room for royalty. At the end of the gauntlet, a little girl, eight years, nine at the most, stood with her hands on her hips, staring at Jim. Her jet-black hair tumbled down into two pigtails and she squinted her eyes, just a bit. Her teeth were a dull white row of uneven chicklets between her lips. "Who are you?" she asked.

"Me?" Jim said.

"Yeah. Who are you?"

"I'm Jim. Uh, Mr. Jim." He was enjoying the game. Tilting his head slightly, he asked, "And who are you?"

"I'm the Princess of the Shelter," she announced.

"She ain't kiddin', Man," someone standing in line said. Others smiled.

"I am very glad to make your acquaintance, madam," Jim said, taking a bow. "I've never met a real princess."

"And why are you here," she said, "in my, um, kingdom?"

She was adorable and disarming. "I'm here to help... I guess I'm really here to learn."

The cute little girl with the uneven teeth and smiling eyes burst out laughing. She ran to him and bear hugged his leg. "You're a good man, Mr. Jim," she said, and he was speechless.

"You can stay," she said as she turned to skip down the hall.

"Wait," Jim said. "I didn't get your name, Princess."

"I'm Princess Tajuana." A woman in her mid-twenties came to stand by her.

"It's an honor to meet you, Princess Tajuana." Her face was all grins. "Say, may I ask you something?"

She nodded.

"Have you ever seen this lady?" he showed the picture of Jean.

"Yeah!" Tajuana said. "She gives me water downtown."

"I'm sorry, Mr. Jim. Tajuana can be a pain, sometimes," the woman said.

"Oh, no. She is wonderful."

"Well, I'll try to keep her outa your way." She placed a hand on the back of the girl's head and steered her away from Jim.

"Excuse me," Jim said. "Tajuana said she knew this woman... my wife." He held up the picture.

"Yeah. I seen her. Most of us here seen her." She eyed him cautiously.

"Good," Jim said. "Unfortunately, she had a stroke a few weeks ago. Some homeless... people helped her, at least that's what the EMTs said. I wanted to thank them."

"I don't know nothin' 'bout that." She turned again. "We gotta get in line or we'll miss supper," she said.

Jim watched them walk down the hall. Tajuana looked over her shoulder at him. "Nice to meet you, Princess Tajuana!"

Her grin broke his heart.

"You won't find what you're searching for, Jim." The center director was standing beside him. "These folks... They don't know what you really want."

"I just want to thank the people who helped Jean."

"You know, the people who helped her might be right here in this room, but they won't let you know. They're afraid you might turn on them... might accuse the people who helped your wife of stealing from her."

"I wouldn't do that..."

"But they don't know you wouldn't. They don't know you. They've been hurt before, so they try to keep to themselves. They like to stay... invisible."

Jim studied his face.

"They find it's safer that way."

CHAPTER FOUR

Yo Jeremy. U got a sec?

Hey Todd. What's up?

Todd hadn't been in contact with his lifelong friend in a long time. After graduation, they had attended separate schools — Todd went to UNC Charlotte and Jeremy to App State. He had heard Jeremy was teaching middle school history in Monroe. He wasn't that far away — maybe thirty minutes — but time and a little distance and a frustrating job can work against friendships.

Todd typed a response. Not much. U?

U know. Same. Dating a great girl. U?

Todd wondered how a nerd like Jeremy could be dating someone, anyone... but great?

Nobody. Was in a long relationship (4 months) but broke up.

Todd paused, wondering what Jeremy might say if he continued... He typed.

I got into trouble. Car accident. Hit a guy on a bike. He died.

There was a long pause as Todd waited for the little dot-dot-dot at the bottom of the screen, indicating Jeremy was replying. Nothing. Maybe Jeremy freaked out.

He was leaning on his elbows, studying the screen, wishing for a reply when his phone jolted him back. Jeremy was calling.

"Man, I can't believe this. You pranking me?"

Todd leaned back in his office chair. "I only wish I was."

"Wow. I had no idea... So what happens next?"

"Court. Since I don't have any priors and I was sober when it happened, my attorney thinks I'll get off with a ton of community service work."

"You're a lucky man, Todd."

"Don't feel lucky."

"Let's grab a beer. Do you wanna meet at Duckworth's?"

It was just around the corner from Todd's apartment. "I can't. I've got volunteer service to do tonight. I'm rewiring our church's speaker system... Hey, did I mention I've joined a church?"

"No. But that could be a good thing..."

"Well, that's exactly what I want, what I need."

"It's not like Gramma Bamma's church, is it?" Concern floated through the phone speaker.

Grandma had lived about twenty miles, and twenty years, away from Charlotte on a farm with cows and pigs and chickens — *Oh My*! His parents often sent him to her farm when they wanted some "us time".

Gramma Bamma's was the worst. The animals made the farm smell putrid and there was no A/C in the house, so he had to sleep with the window open. And there was no internet access.

But the worst thing about Gramma Bamma's house was going to church. Every Sunday she attended a small church in a rickety old wooden building, and when Todd was at the farm, she took him with her. The church begged for fresh paint to replace old flakes of white now covering the walls. Todd made a habit of peeling off a piece or two every time he was there in hopes that the building might one day collapse without its support. The paint, like the architecture and the rickety sign out front bearing the name, "Mt. Pisgah Pentecostal Holiness Church", made it the last place a teenage nerd wanted to be on a Sunday.

The first time he visited with Grandma, it scared the bejesus out of him. It started with the hymns, and people holding their arms up and swaying back and forth. Then came the sermon, with images of fire and pain and evil. But the really scary part was the end when the preacher invited people to respond. Some walked around the church as if in a trance, raising their arms. Many "spoke in tongues," which Grandma said was a special way of talking with God. Their language sounded like something from Arabia, with a southern dialect. That first day, an old man announced, "God is calling the person I touch to repent." He stumbled forward like a guy holding a divining rod searching for water. Todd cringed and tried to force himself into the wood of the old pew beneath him. The zombie-guy stood in front of him and reached over and touched a teenage girl behind him who began to wail and cry, and ran to the front of the church to pray at the altar.

Todd tried everything to avoid going to church with Grandma; feigning sickness, hiding in the attic, refusing to exit the car. Once he even forced his finger down his throat when she wasn't looking and threw up on the kitchen floor. Grandma just said it was proof he needed to go to the church for healing.

Todd began to pray that Grandma would die. When his mother told him she had passed away, he panicked, sure his prayers for his seventy-six year-old grandmother had killed her. He felt sick to his stomach and stayed home from school for two days. On the day of her funeral, he ran away to Jeremy's house where he hid in the basement until that evening. His parents grounded him for a week.

"Like Gramma's church? Hell, no. Nothing like that."

"Good."

"I'm kinda interested in a girl there."

"You dog! I knew it."

"We'll see how it works out." Todd checked the clock at the top of his computer monitor. "Jerr, I gotta run. Volunteer work."

"Keep in touch, okay? That offer for a beer still stands."

"Okay…"

"Remember, Todd. You'll get through this. Be patient, like the citizens of Narnia waiting for Aslan."

Todd disconnected the call shaking his head. *Good ol' Jeremy. Once a nerd, always a nerd.* With Jeremy's voice still an echo, the darkness closed in, again.

• • •

Jim woke up with a fierce, pounding headache exacerbated by loud eruptions of thunder outside. Stumbling into the bathroom he discovered he had no pain relievers in his medicine cabinet. After all, Jean had always stocked the meds and since her death… He returned to the bedroom where he fell back down on the bed and kneaded his temples with his fingers, but the pain would not go away.

Throwing on some sweats and tennis shoes, he grabbed his car keys and went in search of a twenty-four-hour pharmacy. A late-night thunderstorm had not yet begun but threatened to at any moment. Dry lightning foreshadowed the coming downpour. He was unsuccessful in his search for a drugstore, but an all-night gas station offered hope for headache pain relief. He went inside and bought a bottle of water and the last overpriced packet of Acetaminophen in the store.

The glare of the outside floodlights blinded him temporarily. He held his hand above his eyes as he turned the corner to where his Escalade was parked and stumbled over a dingy man leaning against the store wall. "What the..."

The man, reeking of alcohol and cigarettes, rolled over onto his hands and knees. With much effort, he forced himself to stand and without a word, turned to walk away.

"Get on out of here," Jim yelled, seething. His head throbbed with each syllable he spoke.

The man leaned his head to the left and muttered, "Sorry."

"Yeah, you are! You're a sorry piece of crap," Jim yelled, and his head pounded even harder. Then he recalled his recent encounters with the homeless — Gene, the shelter on Tryon, Princess Tajuana, and how some homeless people had helped Jean during her stroke, so he reined in his anger. He ripped the medicine pouch open, and the two pills fell into a puddle of water — or something worse — at his feet. "That's just great!" he yelled. He pounded the hood of his SUV until his fist hurt and broad dents appeared in the metal.

Leaning on the car, he caught his breath and then returned to the store. He bought a six-pack of beer and headed for home, planning to drown the pain with booze. In the recent past he had read about a study that indicated a couple of pints of beer would reduce a migraine headache faster than over-the-counter painkillers. Pulling out of the parking lot, he unscrewed the top of the first bottle and took a deep chug. Two more and the bottle was empty, so he threw it into the floor in front of the passenger seat and sped up the road. He turned his head for an instant while reaching for another bottle and looked up just in time to see a skinny man with a ragged beard step off the curb into his path. Stomping the brake pedal, his SUV swerved to the right and slammed into the concrete curb alongside the road with enough force to rip open the side of his tire.

Jim climbed out of his vehicle and ran around to the passenger side to inspect the damaged and deflated right front tire as rain began to pummel the pavement. A gaping tear appeared in the side of the all-weather tire. The vagrant who had stepped into the street in front of him was nowhere to be found.

His shoulders seemed to grow heavy, as if they were sponges that soaked up the rain beating down, causing them to grow heavier and heavier. He couldn't stop them from sagging. His feet felt cemented to the asphalt as the rain fell harder.

In the glare of LED headlights, Jim's arms rose as if buoyed by the puddles of water on the street around him in acceptance of the encumbering darkness. Arms outstretched as if to hold up the entire world, Jim breathed in the wet evening air and breathed out complete surrender.

He sensed a presence behind him before he saw the flashing red and blue lights on the backs of his eyelids. A tinny-sounding voice broke through the pounding rain, "This is the Charlotte-Mecklenburg County Police. Slowly turn around."

Jim complied.

The officer stepped out of the car and shined his brilliant flashlight on Jim. "Sir," he called. "Lower your arms."

Again, Jim obeyed.

The officer approached him, told him he was going to search him, and then patted him down. As he did, he had Jim explain the circumstances that brought Jim to be standing, arms outstretched in the rain. Too exhausted for tears, Jim described his wife's recent death and the grief that followed, the mugging in uptown Charlotte and his futile efforts to move on.

A second officer searched inside Jim's car. "Out for a night on the town?" the policeman asked.

"I had a killer headache and went out to find some medicine."

"But you bought beer, instead?"

"They were out."

"Uh-huh."

"Officer. I seldom drink. I only had one bottle, and I'm heading home right now."

The cop examined his license and said, "Your house isn't very far away."

"No. Just down to the next block and then around the corner."

The officer stepped back and surveyed Jim's crippled Escalade. He pointed to a nearby strip mall. "Tell you what. Carefully drive your vehicle to that parking lot and leave it there for the night. We'll take you home and you can pick it up in the morning."

"No problem, sir."

The policeman returned to his vehicle and Jim got in his car and slowly edged it into the parking lot. The cruiser stayed close behind him. After locking his car doors, Jim approached the police car and the officer held the back door open for him to enter. They drove to his house, stopping in front of his driveway. Jim exited the car, entered his house, and plopped onto his lounge chair cursing himself. There he sat immobile until morning.

• • •

A busy day in the emergency room. An afternoon pileup on I-485 sent three ambulances to Wesley Memorial and the team performed in its usual exemplary manner. Chaotic, but exemplary.

Angela had a moment to catch her breath.

Slumping down in a plastic chair in the break room with a diet drink on the table in front of her, she took her cell phone from her purse — her usual routine during her short recess. She noticed she had missed a call. Few people bothered her during work hours and this one might be an emergency call from Emma. Since Angela was working late, her daughter had planned to stay at Pam Reynold's house. Again.

When she read the notice on her phone indicating the source of the message, she tightened up like a spring on a bear trap. She tapped the icon to retrieve the voice message.

"Angela, this is Kayla, Evan's wife." Of course she knew who Kayla was — the woman who'd stolen her husband and ruined her life. "Say, we were wondering if Emma could stay over at our house tonight. I know it's not her regular weekend with her dad, but we're having our new neighbors over for dinner, and they have a daughter who's also an eighth grader, and we thought she and Emma would get along so well. I sent a text to Emma's phone and we'll pick her up after school. Then she can come back to your house after school tomorrow. Okay? By-ee."

Angela ground her teeth and set her phone on the table and worked to steady her breath. Leaning back in her chair, she clasped her fingers together in a bundle of constraint. If she couldn't separate her hands, she wouldn't be tempted to strangle the next person who walked through the breakroom door.

She knew better than to think she could stop Kayla's plan. No doubt, Emma was already on her way to Kayla's house. The only thing now was damage control. Another deep breath and she picked up her phone to call Pam Reynolds.

"Hey, Pam," Angela said. "I'm sorry to do this, but Emma's step-mother is going to take her again this evening. I would have called earlier, but I just got the message."

"No problem," Pam said. "Taylor talked with Emma at school and told me about it when I picked her up. We're all good." Her words were reassuring. "Are you?"

"Don't go there. If I get started, I'll get so mad I'll start yanking catheters around here."

"Well, I don't want that."

"I really do appreciate your support. I don't know what I'd do without a friend like you."

"It's nothing. I'm just concerned," Pam said. "Say, Angie. I do have a question for you, that is if you have a moment."

"Sure. What's up?"

"Well, I don't want to bother you. I know how hard you work at the hospital."

"That's okay."

"I... You... The last time Emma was over, I thought I saw something... Does she have a tattoo?"

"Ha. My God, no. A tattoo?" *Where would she get a tattoo? Why would she do that? Is she hanging around with the wrong crowd?*

"Well, I didn't think..."

"Why do you ask?"

"Well, when she and Taylor were having dinner... she was wearing one of those long sleeve sweatshirts, you know, the kind kids wear these days, with a hood?... and as she was reaching for a bowl... mashed potatoes, I believe... well, I thought I saw some marks on her forearm."

"Are you sure?"

"No, not completely, but I thought I saw some red lines or stripes. A flag?"

"That's weird. I can't imagine."

"Yes, you're probably right," Pam said.

"Besides, it's not legal for a minor to receive a tattoo." Angela could picture an early teen in some dark, sleazy tattoo parlor, grimacing as a long-haired freak scarred her arm with a menacing-looking tattoo gun.

"Maybe it's one of those temporary tattoos. I saw a show about them on TV and they look very realistic."

"That just doesn't sound like Emma. I'll ask her about it tomorrow."

With that, they ended the call and Angela pushed the idea of skin discoloration to the back of her mind for the rest of the shift.

⋅ ⋅ ⋅

She knew it would be cold. Real cold.

On nights like this, the shelters were packed solid. Lines stretched down the street. Food was usually scarce.

But she needed to be safe. For the baby.

It was common for shelter volunteers to move women, particularly pregnant women, to the front of the line, but tonight, like most real cold nights, there were more women than usual. And she wasn't showing as much as some of the others. She tried to stand up straight, to stick out her bulge as much as possible. If they saw she was pregnant, they might move her inside.

An elderly lady with a kind smile tapped her on the shoulder, "Why don't you go up to the front?"

She accepted the offer.

The shelter was crowded with dirty and smelly people. Shelters always were. This particular place had mattresses on the floor. Some only had floor space. She found a mattress in the far dark corner of the large room and set her small canvas tote bag at one end. She had taken it from a grocery store a long time ago. The handles were frayed and one threatened to tear away. She emptied the bag: a light sweater, a plastic rain hat, a pair of dirty socks, and... It was gone! She'd had it that morning, but now the LG cell phone, several years old, was not in her bag. She didn't have an account — few of her friends did, and her phone was useless for making calls. But in shelters like this, or just outside of people's houses, or in the library, she could pick up a Wi-Fi signal and send emails to the few friends she had. She could also read the news, but usually didn't because it made her sad. Mostly, the phone was something to have, to make her feel a little connected.

But now the phone, the charger, and the earbuds were gone. She thought back... That morning, hoping for a throw-away breakfast in the back of Denny's with some others... someone must have snatched it. It would be hard to get along without, but that was all she could do 'til she found another. Sometimes, they gave them away at the shelters. Not tonight. Too many people and not enough phones.

Her growling stomach told her she needed to eat. She had to take care of her baby. She'd never let her go and they could never take her away... She could lose it... Like she lost Danielle...

A short wiry man stood beside the kitchen window. He explained the rules and made a couple of announcements. Some of the people wandered to the food line and accepted plates of spaghetti, apple sauce, bread and a slice of cake. Others returned to their beds to finish setting up for the night.

She took her plate to a table near the doorway and quickly devoured the contents. Someone came by with bags of soap, shampoo, a toothbrush and a small tube of toothpaste. She had lost her last toothbrush over a week ago. She took the gift and stuffed it into the bottom of her bag, glad to receive a new one. After she finished, she left her plate with a volunteer and went back to the sleeping area.

Sitting cross-legged on the thin mattress, she looked around the room. They kept the lights low to help people sleep. In the morning they turned them up to get people going. A lady two beds away was snoring. A few people drifted to another room to watch a basketball game on TV.

Others poured cups of coffee and juice at a table in the hallway. Nobody said much. Nothing to say.

She reached back into her bag, took out the toiletries, and walked down the hall to the women's room. She liked this shelter. They had showers. She waited in line until one of the individual stalls opened and then hurried inside. The water wasn't warm, but it was wet and clean. She hadn't had a shower in a week, maybe two. She dried off with a clean shelter towel and dressed in the same jeans, same flannel shirt, same semi-clean socks, and worn out tennis shoes.

Some men, leaning against the wall in the hallway, leered as she returned to the women's sleeping room. They didn't care if she was pregnant or not. They just wanted to see what they could get.

At her bed, she straightened her belongings again and lay down beneath the provided blanket. The darkness made it easy to drift off. Better than the nights outside when the moon was big and full and bright and the streetlights shown 'til dawn.

A woman on the mattress inches to her right whispered, "Good night."

"G'night," Sheryl said.

On his first full night volunteering at the shelter, Jim arrived early, anxious to help any way he could. The sharp odor of urine and disinfectant permeated everything in the building, but nobody seemed to notice. Jim couldn't un-smell it. It was as if someone had painted the inside of his nostrils and the back of his throat with the obnoxious scent.

He checked in at the volunteers' desk and went searching for Princess Tajuana, the cute little girl who had confronted him on his initial visit, but she and her mother were not there. The center director said people tended to move about from shelter to shelter and even town to town, so it wasn't uncommon to have a lot of turnover among the guests.

The phrase, "structured pandemonium," came to mind as he watched about twenty volunteers rush throughout the building. Some carried pans of food — spaghetti or garlic bread. Others handed out plastic bags containing little bottles of shampoo, toothbrushes and toothpaste. "Here comes the sock man," one of the guests yelled and heads turned to a man wearing an Atlanta Braves baseball cap and a shirt containing the logo of a local sports store. He passed out packages of athletic socks to anyone who would take them.

Jim sat with some big, burly guys at dinner time. A couple of them had played football in high school, and one had played a year in college. Since the Super Bowl was coming up, they talked nonstop about the game. DeWayne Johnson said he knew a couple of players on the Panthers and predicted they would guarantee a Carolina victory. Little Jimmy Patton, the youngest in the group, boasted he had been to five Super Bowls. Red Fred said he had been reading up on Super Bowls and lamented the fact that the Steelers weren't in this year's Bowl, having won more titles than any other team.

DeWayne was halfway through a story about how he'd ruined his right knee in a game, ending his football career, when Rev. Allen Rhodes walked through the doors of the dining hall. All eyes at Jim's table turned to him. "Now that's a badass preacher man," said the guy sporting a seventies-era fu manchu.

"What? Why do you say that?"

"When he was a kid, he was a champion boxer."

"That good?"

"Best in the Southeast."

The man sitting across the table from Jim said, "I heard of him when I was a young 'un. I lived in Atlanta, and Allen Rhodes was easily the best in the city. Three years' running."

Allen strolled over to their table, fist-bumped the guests and pulled up a chair. "Jim Bishop," he said. "I see you've met some of my friends."

"If these guys are your friends, then you're in good company."

A couple of hours later, after nonstop smack talk about players, coaches, and teams, the guests turned in for the night and Jim and Allen talked in low voices over hot chocolate.

"How'd you get involved with this outfit?" Allen asked.

Jim explained how he decided to seek out and thank the homeless people who had helped Jean during her stroke.

"Sounds like what Jean would do," Allen said.

A flash of memory and Jim knew he was right. "All the time." He rubbed his hands together between his knees. "A couple of weeks ago I went into the city to give some blankets to homeless people, hoping to find the people who'd helped Jean."

"Really? How'd that work out?"

Jim pointed to a bruise on his forehead. "I got mugged."

Allen flinched. "I'd wondered what had happened."

Jim shook his head and studied his shoes. "Have you ever been mugged?" It was more of a prod to confirm whether Allen was indeed the badass the Manchu guy said.

"No, but when I was a kid I learned to take care of myself." Muscles strained against his blue golf shirt and the fabric hugged his upper chest. "But," Allen continued, "I think you might be onto something. Your blanket mission sounds like a good idea."

"I'm not so sure. A cop told me to just donate the blankets to charity and let them give them out."

Allen nodded. "Well, that's what they do and they do it well." He leaned back in his chair.

"So, long story short, I came back into the city, stumbled upon this place, and was impressed with their operation. I bought into it."

"Good for you. Charlotte Homeless Shelter is a good organization. They need all the volunteers they can get, so thank you for helping."

"What about you? What's your connection?"

"I started working with the director and his crew when we moved here about five years ago. Somehow, he recruited me to be on his board, so I help whenever I can. Tonight I'm just dropping by for support." Allen said he hadn't intended to stay the night, so he thanked Jim for his help again and slipped out the back door.

Jim had chosen to stay overnight. Many of the other volunteers had family or other obligations that made overnight stays difficult, but he didn't have a problem with the schedule. About eleven o'clock, he patrolled the center to be sure everyone had whatever they needed. Most of them were asleep. One other volunteer was awake — a short man with messy blond hair trimmed close on the side. His clothes, gray t-shirt and blue jeans, hung on him like a drape.

Jim sat next to him in the hall. "How ya holding up?"

"Bored. Tired, I guess."

"Name's Jim Bishop." He extended his hand.

"Todd Sanders."

They both stared at the beige concrete blocks on the other side of the hallway.

"So, what prompted you to volunteer to stay up all night at a homeless shelter?" Jim asked.

The young man — he was half Jim's age, but with the fatigue in his eyes of someone much older — sighed like he was breathing his last breath. "This is part of my community service."

"Yeah?"

"A few months ago, I was in an accident... I hit a guy on his bicycle... late at night... a rainy night. Well, I plead guilty, but since I wasn't drinking and didn't have a record, I was sentenced to community service. I was lucky, I guess. The cyclist was a donor to this shelter, and the judge thought I should serve some of my community service time here."

Jim hung his head. "Wow. That's tough."

"Yeah, but it could have been much worse. I could be in prison."

"Yeah. The judge must have been looking out for you. Still, I imagine this has been a rough time."

"You have no idea. I lost fifty pounds. My hair was falling out, so I cut it short. But my church has been there for me, at least, so far."

Jim looked up and down the hallway as if searching for some other topic. "It's kinda quiet tonight."

"Yeah. These folks just want a place to rest. This is an easy gig for volunteers."

"Where do you work when you're not here?" Jim asked.

"I'm a programmer with Bell Intelliservices."

"No way! I used to work there, retired a couple of years ago. Good company."

Todd raised a single eyebrow in dissent.

"How is Bell doing?" Jim asked.

"It's a tech mill now — they grind you up and spit you out." He raised his head. "But at least I've still got a job."

They were an odd pair — an older guy searching for some homeless people he'd never met and a young kid seeking redemption.

A quiet had settled over the hall. The only sound came from where DeWayne Johnson slept. In a while the rhythmic rumble of his snoring made Jim sleepy, so he said goodnight to Todd and retired to the volunteer's room for the night.

. . .

The next morning, Jim woke up before most of the men in the shelter and headed, stiff and sore, to the kitchen to help a new crew of volunteers serve breakfast. Todd was there, setting out plates and plasticware.

"Hey, Bud," Jim said, slapping him on the shoulder. "How'd you sleep?"

He shook his head. "Couldn't. I don't sleep much these days." With such guilt weighing down on him, it was a wonder he ever slept.

After most of the guests had finished breakfast, Jim was wiping down the tables when he saw the pregnant lady at the back of the hall. Head down, she shoveled food into her mouth like a starving prisoner, which she kind of was. He guessed she must be four or five months along, but her shoulders and arms were so thin he couldn't tell for sure. He pulled up a chair opposite her.

"Hi."

She didn't look up.

"My name's Jim."

She continued to shove scrambled eggs into her mouth with a spoon.

"What's your name."

Her skinny hand froze in mid air. Then, in a soft voice, almost a prayer, "Sheryl."

Jim couldn't decide if he should leave her alone or press on with small talk. She ate the eggs on her spoon.

"Tell me, Sheryl. Tell me about yourself."

Her hands stopped again, inches from her mouth. A clump of buttered grits threatened to slip off her spoon and fall back to the plate. "Ain't much to tell."

"Everybody's got a story. What's yours?"

She shook her head.

"Got a family? Husband?"

She shook her head, again.

"Sisters? Brothers?"

She shook her head once more. "Gonna have a baby, soon."

"Yeah? Tell me about your baby."

"Don't know who the daddy is. Lots of men 'round here do whatever they want."

"Do you know how far along you are?"

She shook her head.

"Have you seen a doctor? Any prenatal care?"

"Can't 'ford it." She pushed the grits into her mouth.

Jim thought that might be a sign she was warming up to him. "I'm sure there must be a free health clinic somewhere around here. I'll bet the center director might be able to make a recommendation. I'll even drive you there."

She shook her head faster this time. "Can't. They'll take my baby."

Her answer surprised him. "Take your baby?"

"Uh, huh. They take mamas' babies."

"I don't think they can do that... Not without your permission."

She spooned up some more eggs. "They take people's babies."

Jim leaned back. He didn't know anything about community healthcare or pregnancy. It might be better for Sheryl to talk with a woman. He scanned the hall for a female volunteer.

Too late. Sheryl finished her cup of coffee and stood to go.

When Jim reached across the table to collect her place setting, their hands touched and she jerked hers back. She said nothing but turned away.

"See you later, Sheryl," Jim called. She appeared to whisper to herself as she weaved through empty chairs and tables toward the door.

CHAPTER FIVE

It was early afternoon when the phone rang at the church office. "Allen." Concern clouded his wife's voice. "You need to come home. Now."

"Grace, I'm right in the middle of research for Sunday's Sermon..."

"Now, Allen."

Pulling into the garage, he noticed Paul's car was not in the driveway. Paul, a sixteen-going on-twenty-one-year-old, was the prodigal son in a family without a good one — a black sheep in a herd of one. Grace and Allen had struggled with him over the last couple of years. It started with missed classes. One or two, here or there, turned into five or ten. He'd stayed out late — first on weekends and then several nights a week. Allen assumed there was a girl involved... someone who had seduced him into belligerency, but when he skipped prom, they decided there was no girl. Assuming this crisis was not about Paul, Allen relaxed... a bit. But relaxing wasn't his strong suit.

"Follow me," Grace said as she turned toward the bedrooms in the back. He fell in line behind her. Paul's bed looked like it had never been made, sports posters decked out the walls, and the desk was cluttered, except for the blank space where his laptop sat when it was not in his backpack at school.

"I was vacuuming and found this under his bed." She held a College-Ruled Composition notebook in both hands. Black and white splotches marbled the front, and a black strip of cloth secured the binding.

Accepting the notebook as if she were handing him a grenade, Allen opened it at the front, sure to find images of porn, or phone numbers of girls, or words of lament. "White Lives Matter" leapt at him from the first page. Beneath it, a picture of Paul, hand up, displaying what some would assume was an "OK" sign, a secret "White Power" symbol, made Allen cringe. A drawing of a confederate flag appeared on the second, above the words, "The South WILL Rise Again." He flipped through the notebook. Phrases like, "White Pride", "Deport Immigrants, Now!" and "Pure White as the Virgin Snow," accompanied derogatory comments about Muslims, Jews, and Blacks. A gray swastika with red drops of blood dripping from the points of the symbol covered another page, followed by printed photos of Dylan Roof, Wade Michael Page, Daniel Cowart, Patrick Crusius, and half a dozen other extremists, several with shaved heads, all wild-eyed and furious. More than one seemed to sneer in defiance at the camera.

He longed to close the book but couldn't take his eyes from it, as if seeing the contents would make them go away. His fist clenched so tight his fingernails bit into his palms. *My son. Oh, God. What has he gotten into?* Allen needed to close the notebook. Its presence choked his mind; he couldn't think. The media, his congregation, other ministers would turn on him if they found out about this book. He slammed it shut, But the images remained branded in his memory.

His knees felt weak and he sat back onto the bed... the place his son slept every night... his sanctuary. He thought he knew Paul — probably better than anyone else in the world — but now his son seemed like the most distant foreigner. He was a stranger, not to welcome, but to fear.

"That's not all," Grace said in a low voice. She reached to the desk beside her and lifted a hand towel, unveiling a pistol. "This was under his mattress."

Allen couldn't move. He couldn't touch it. If he did, he would know for sure it was authentic. It remained lying on the desk, unmoved, unreal.

Grace placed a soft, comforting hand on his shoulder. "How can this be? He knows how we feel..."

Breathing was coming hard now. Clasping sweaty hands over his belly, he remained silent, closing his eyes to shut out reality. He found little comfort in denial.

"He's heard you preach about race a thousand times."

He moved his hands to his forehead, kneading his flesh to drive away the painful ache in his skull.

"We've had people from every race and every religious group in our house. We've broken bread..." Her hand squeezed harder on Allen's shoulder.

Allen reached up and placed his hand over hers. He opened his eyes to the things around the room — a championship wrestling trophy Paul had won two years ago, twisting like an eel to avoid being pinned, a snow globe celebrating his visit to Florida in the sixth grade, and a wooden framed photograph of the three of them taken three summers ago before he went to camp. A low moan emerged from his pained chest. "We'll talk to him tonight after dinner."

Grace said nothing but stood by, cupping his shoulder with her hand.

"Let me be alone for awhile, Grace."

She kissed him on his cheek and left the room.

In the waning light in Paul's room, a distant, but powerful memory flooded his soul. Politeness had been drilled into him during childhood. His father, and to a lesser extent, his mother, constantly reminded him to say, "Sir," and "Ma'am," when addressing grownups. He treated teachers with respect, never interrupting or being rude. He stood when adults entered the room, held doors open for women, and showed high regard for everyone.

Well, almost everyone.

One night during his junior year of high school, before his call to the ministry, he and a few of his friends were walking through a neighborhood on the south side of Atlanta. "White flight" had hit the community hard, leaving behind a neighborhood of minorities. Allen's basketball team had just suffered a severe trouncing by the local high school, and Allen and his friends were feeling angry and seeking revenge. At a small, dingy convenience store, they slipped a twenty to the guy behind the counter and bought a couple of six packs, which only served to embolden the boys more.

Alcohol and anger had clouded their minds and talks of retribution enflamed their spirits as they made their way to the Marta subway station. They passed a small park where a couple of kids, middle schoolers at best, were shooting hoops. It took no time for the white gang to pounce. Allen did the most damage. A local Golden Gloves champ, he knew where to punch to leave the most damage. With his left hand clenched around the boy's collar he was pummeling the helpless kid in the face with his right, when the boy gurgled through broken teeth and lips, "What'd we do to you, Man? What'd we do?"

Allen stopped mid-swing as the boy's words blasted through his rage and alcohol-inflamed thoughts. He let go of the boy's collar and walked away.

From that day forward, he eschewed racism and bigotry. But now his son had embraced a view far more severe than Allen's had been. The sins of the father...

The past, the present, the frightening future rushed in to crush his soul. His son was in trouble.

The ache in his heart erupted. *Please, God. Help him.*

Allen wept.

⁕ ⁕ ⁕

Pushing himself back against the rough faux brick wall that encased Bell's I.T. Department, Todd peeked out the window. He ignored the heat of the coffee in his paper cup, even though it threatened to scald his hand. Down below, near the bus stop with its clear, plexiglass roof, a figure wearing a gray hooded jacket stood motionless. Short, wiry. He was sure — almost sure — he'd seen the same guy before, back at his apartment.

A chance glance out his living room window one evening revealed a lone figure peering behind a tree. Even though he was fifty yards away, Todd could make out the silhouette — a short, skinny guy wearing a hoodie, like the urban gangbangers in the movies. Todd stepped closer to the glass door and slid it open wide. The figure jumped behind the tree and stayed there for at least five minutes. Then, the figure slipped away, skirting the amber dome of the streetlight and fading into the evening blackness.

He was sure it was the same person. Sweat dampened his armpits. Since the accident, Todd's state of mind, his "normal", hadn't just shifted — it had evaporated altogether.

Another coder stepped up to the window. "What's up?"

"Get outa the way." Todd pushed him to the other side of the window. "That guy. Down there by the bus stop. Wearing the hoodie."

The engineer moved back in front of the window. "So what?"

The strange guy was like the Crebain in the Fangorn Forest of Middle Earth, spying on everybody. Todd leaned over to check up and down the street, trying to recognize others among the pedestrian. "I've seen 'em before."

"Yeah. Me, too. It's like he's all over the city," he mocked. "Everybody wears hoodies these days."

Todd ignored him, convinced the guy down below was stalking him.

A full-sized bus sporting the CATS logo pulled up next to the curb. "There," the programmer said. "He's leaving."

After the bus drove off, Todd kept staring at the plexiglass structure below in case the guy reappeared from behind a tree, or a post, or from thin air. Crebain sometimes seemed to do that.

The engineer moved back to his desk and Todd turned away as well. In his cube he sipped his coffee, preparing to gaze at his screen for another hour. Letters, graphics, screen dumps all turned blurry. The sound of the phone beside his monitor jolted him awake. It rang again. Stretching a shaky hand toward the device, he lifted the receiver from the cradle. "Todd Sanders..."

"Oh, I'm sorry. Dialed the wrong extension," a voice said, and the phone went dead. Todd returned the handset to the cradle and leered at the device as if it was a bomb.

"How's the project coming along?" Ron, standing behind him, asked. He had a weird habit of sneaking up on employees at the worst time.

"Oh, uh, good," Todd said, wondering how long he'd been standing there. Todd placed his left hand on the keyboard and moved his right hand to the mouse. The pointer danced across the screen.

"Okay. Let me know if you have any questions. We're still shooting to finish tomorrow." He left Todd's cube and advanced to the programmer at the next station. "Looks good, Steve."

Todd shook his head once and tried to focus on the code before him.

• • •

A deep gray, overcast sky announced the coming of another cold night. Jim found himself more easily irritated these days. Just a few minutes outside helped to center him. A quick walk in the cold made him appreciate the warmth of his house. Bundled up in his overcoat and scarf he followed his regular route to Independence Park on Charlotteville Avenue for fresh air and an attitude adjustment. Hawthorne Lane led to the lower section with its rose garden and towering trees where he settled onto a bench beside a tranquil reflecting pond and... reflected. When he was a Boy Scout, he loved the water, especially swimming and canoeing with his friends. Something about the water and the woods challenged and soothed him. He collected swimming and canoeing merit badges on his way to achieving his Eagle Scout rank.

He felt close to Jean here. She had once told him she liked this park. He regretted not coming with her more often, but something always seemed to get in the way. In retrospect, late afternoon meetings, Saturday afternoon naps, and NFL football games were wastes of time. The sun shimmered on the water and he thought of these things knowing Jean never resented him for not joining on her trips to the park. She was like that.

A loud, high-pitched bark, and then a black Scottish Terrier, long hair flapping beneath his muzzle, burst through his thoughts. The dog bounded down the path toward his bench and took two laps around Jim before hopping up onto the seat beside him. Jim reached over to the pup and the wriggling dog allowed his ears to be scratched. A circular tag clung to the leather collar around his neck, monogrammed with the letters, "J.B."

"Here, boy!" A child, no more than seven, dashed up the trail dragging a short leash, to where Jim and the dog were sitting. "Where have you been?" He stopped at the bench and grasped the dog's collar. "Come on. Grandma's looking for us."

"It's okay," Jim said. "He just stopped to say hello."

"Do you like dogs?"

"I like this one," Jim said. "I saw the tag on his collar. Is his name J.B."

"No. Those are just his initials."

"Those are my initials, too. I'm Jim Bishop."

"I'm Mike," the boy said, trying to drag the stubborn pet from the bench.

"So, what do the initials stand for?"

"His name. Jackson Browne."

"Jackson Browne?"

"Yeah. My grandma gave him to me. She named him after some singer."

A woman emerged from the same trail as the boy. She wore a pink jogging suit with the words, "Grandma's 4.5K Run" adorning the front and a baseball cap with a red ponytail flowing behind. She seemed a bit mature for the cute cap and a little young for the oversized sweats. "I am so sorry to have bothered you," she said to Jim as she approached the bench. Her makeup was subtly stylish — noticeable but not too gaudy. She looked familiar...

Jim stood. "Oh, no bother at all. He's a very polite young man."

Mike grabbed Jackson's leash, hooked it to the dog's collar, and the two ran toward the pond, no doubt avoiding embarrassing grownup talk.

"Not too close to the water," his grandmother called.

"You know, your dog has the same initials as I do. I'm Jim Bishop." He extended his hand, and she welcomed it with hers.

"My name's Peggy Crutchfield." Her eyes glimmered in the afternoon sunlight.

"You seem familiar. Have we met?"

"Maybe. I'm pretty active these days."

"The grocery store? A coffee shop?"

"Maybe. In addition to taking care of Michael, I also volunteer at the hospital."

Jim snapped his fingers. "Wesley Memorial? That's it. I've seen you at the information desk. I've been there a couple of times recently. The staff at the hospital was very supportive."

Sarah nodded and smiled softly. "We all try to be helpful. And you wouldn't believe the things I've seen and heard since I've been volunteering." She smiled. "Of course, we're always seeking more volunteers. If you have the time..."

"Thank you. I'll keep that in mind." Jim, not ready to make any more commitments, changed the subject. "Cute kid," he said, nodding toward Mike, who was running along the shore of the pond.

"Michael is such a good boy." She folded her hands in her lap. "We get to spend a lot of time together, since my husband passed a year ago."

"I'm sorry to hear..."

"Oh, no, I'm sorry. I just can't seem to stop talking about it." She touched his arm lightly. "You'd think by now I'd get used to it. He died a year ago — oh, I already said that... cancer... kidney cancer."

Jim shook his head.

"Renal cell carcinoma, they called it. It's supposed to be fairly rare for someone in his early fifties."

"That must have been a difficult time," Jim said. "I know it's tough. I lost my wife to a stroke a couple of months ago."

They talked about their experiences and then watched the boy and the dog chase each other on the park lawn.

"I like the name, 'Jackson Browne,'" Jim said. "He's one of my favorites. But you know, the singer doesn't look anything like that dog." He grinned.

She smiled.

"Well, I really must be getting them both home. I sit with him most afternoons while his mother's at work."

"She's lucky to have you so close by."

"Oh, it's such a pleasure for me. Michael gives me so much joy. Since I've been single, I don't have a lot to keep me busy." She stood, clapped her hands, and called the boy and his dog. "Maybe we'll see each other again. We come here two or three times a week."

"That would be nice." He stood to say goodbye. "I enjoyed meeting you, Ms. Crutchfield, and Mike, and Jackson Browne."

"Please call me Peggy," she said over her shoulder as she moved to catch up with her grandson. "Bye, Mr. Jim," Mike called.

Jim waved, breathed in the healthy cool air, and turned back toward his house. It was good to talk with someone, even though Peggy seemed a little younger than he. New friends were important.

. . .

Dinner was anything but usual.

Allen's gut felt constricted, as if his torso was in the grip of a boa constrictor, squeezing the life from him. He ate little. Grace fidgeted with her spaghetti, swirling it around on her fork and letting it slip back down to the plate. She drank a lot of water.

Paul helped clear the table like a normal kid who would never possess such a vile notebook, to say nothing of a gun. After the dishes were placed in the dishwasher, Allen asked his son to join them in the living room. Paul raised one eyebrow, but obediently followed his parents.

"Paul," Allen said after the three had settled. "We found your notebook."

"What notebook?"

Allen thought he saw a flicker in his eyes. "You know what notebook. The one with the racist drawings and words."

Paul's eyes opened wide. His nostrils flared. "What were you doing in my room?"

"I was cleaning up," Grace said.

"Why were you snooping around in my stuff? You have no right."

"We have every..." Grace said, but Allen cut her off. Arguing about rights was just a distraction, and a defensive one at that. "Where did you get this garbage?"

Paul turned his face away from his mother and to his father. "What garbage?"

"The idea that one race is better than others. That murderers like Dylann Roof and Robert Bowers are to be... idolized. They killed ministers... Rabbis... church members..."

"It's everywhere," Paul said. "Everybody says things like that."

"No, not everybody."

"They do in my school," he said, jutting his chin.

"Who?"

"You don't know them."

"Paul," Grace interrupted. "We love you. We know what's in that notebook is not you."

"Maybe it is."

"You're better than that."

"That's my point. That's our point. We are better. Whites are better. Your Bible teaches that. The Jews were 'chosen'," he said with air quotes. "They failed. Now, anglos are 'chosen'." Air quotes again.

"Listen, Paul. When I was younger, I made a lot of mistakes... hurt a lot of people. But, even then, I knew this... this kind of garbage was wrong."

"That was a long time ago. Things are different, now."

Allen surveyed the young man's face. His chin was chiseled and his cheeks had grown firm, but his eyes were still those of the boy he picked up at summer camp, who played T-Ball with kids of all races, who once said his middle school biology teacher — a black man — was his favorite. *Where did he go?* He breathed a deep breath, knowing he had to think and avoid getting emotional. "You know Christians don't believe that. We taught you better. Your faith..."

"Maybe," Paul said, narrowing his eyes into a laser-like stare. "Maybe I don't want to be a Christian."

Allen's mind locked up, as did his throat. He had failed his own son.

"Paul," Grace said, almost a whisper. "We also found the gun."

"What? Give it back." He stood. Threatening to fight, or to run away?

"We can't," Allen said, feeling defeated. "We turned it over to the police," he lied. He no longer cared if he told the truth or not. His fists tightened.

"What? You turned... You took my property? And you call yourselves Christian..."

"Yes, we do," Allen said in a softer voice.

"We did it to protect you," Grace offered, continuing the lie.

"You did it to protect yourselves," Paul quipped. "What would the people in your church say if they knew your precious son had a pistol."

Allen took another tack. "Paul, what would you do if you were us?"

"I'd leave my son alone and let him make his own decisions." He stood.

"You know we can't do that. Not in this situation."

"Well, that's what you should do. I'm not a baby anymore." He stood, backed away from them, bumping into a table, knocking a lamp that had been Allen's mother's to the floor, where it broke into several ceramic chunks.

But the lamp wasn't important. Not now.

Paul turned, stepping on pieces of broken lamp and marched toward his room at the back of the house. The door slammed.

The silence in the living room was a welcome relief from the noise of battle. It was also hell. Grace reached over to take Allen's hand in hers. He sought her eyes, breathed his shoulders erect, and told her, "We will get through this."

"I know."

CHAPTER SIX

Head low so no one would notice, Todd moved toward the elevator. They all knew about the accident. They all stared these days. He wanted to fade into the mirrors that lined the elevator lobby and become just an image of himself.

He usually ate lunch early — about eleven o'clock — so he could eat alone. Then he'd be back at his desk while everyone else was taking their lunch breaks at restaurants, sports bars, or the nearby food trucks. Walking out the front door with his head down, he almost ran into a broad-shouldered man wearing a dark blue suit and mis-matched green tie. Todd said nothing.

"Hey. I know you," the man said.

Todd looked up at the man, not in his eyes or at his face even, but at the nondescript entity before him.

"Todd, right?" The man extended his right hand. "I'm Jim Bishop... from the homeless shelter the other night."

"Oh... Yeah... Right." He shook the man's large, strong hand.

"Where you headin'?" Jim asked.

"I'm just going to grab a sandwich at the food truck."

"Mind if I join you? I haven't eaten lunch yet."

Todd shrugged. He really didn't want company, preferring to just grab a wrap and get back to his cube where he could zone out at his desk and act kinda busy. Better than having to talk to anyone else from Bell.

The food truck was like every food truck parked around facilities that contained large numbers of hungry employees. Faded signs along the sides announced the availability of wraps, sandwiches, drinks, and chips. Owning a food truck might be much better than programming. At least he wouldn't be hounded by his boss and every boss wanna-be in the office. 'Course he might still be hounded by the stalker in the gray hoodie. He surveyed the shiny silver van, wondering how easy it might be to hit another bicyclist while driving such a big vehicle on some of Charlotte's skinnier streets. Tangy smells wafted from the truck, reminding him of the old uptown diner where he used to go with his friends... back when he had friends. No one was waiting in line, which was how Todd preferred it these days.

The two men sat at a little round concrete table near the side door of the office and munched on chips and wraps. A gentle breeze rippled the umbrella overhead. "So, how ya been?" the older man asked.

"Fine. 'Bout the same." A mosaic of color stones was embedded in the concrete table.

"Will I see you at the shelter again this week?"

Todd shrugged. The old guy's eyes seemed to be trying to lock onto his own, but he couldn't return the gaze for more than a second or two. "Yeah."

"Wednesday night?"

"Yeah." The questions sounded like an interrogation. "The court commands."

Jim smiled. "You know, the court order thing... I know you have to be at the shelter, but don't lose sight of the fact that you're doing some good there. Those people need your help."

The pattern of the color stones in the tabletop looked monotonous, like the old man's conversation. Sadness turned to frustration and to anger in mere seconds. "You know what, dude? I don't really care about your opinion. You asked to eat lunch with me. I don't give a damn if I'm doing some good at the shelter. I'm just doin' what I have to do. Far as I'm concerned, you can take your do-gooder attitude and cram it."

"Woa! I'm sorry, Man. I didn't mean anything. I know things must really be tough for you, and I just wanted you to know some of us at the shelter appreciate your help. I'm sorry I bothered you." He stood to go.

Todd felt his face heat up. He'd slipped up. "I'm sorry. I shouldn't have gotten mad. I haven't gotten any sleep lately, and little things seem to set me off."

Jim sat back down. "I get it," Jim said. "I apologize if I'm being too pushy. I'm new at this volunteer stuff."

"Me, too."

Jim took another bite of his sandwich. With a nod to the office building beside them, Jim asked, "How's work going?"

"Fine, 'bout the same." He smiled.

Both men chuckled.

"Actually, it's been kinda tough. Work's piling up. I just can't get into it."

Jim shook his head.

"It'll be okay. I've just gotta focus."

"That can be hard to do, sometimes. You may remember, I used to work here. In fact, I'm going up to meet with Ms. Noland in a few minutes, if she has time. I don't know if I have any credibility anymore. But I'll be glad to put in a good word..."

The breeze slipped through the trees above and Jim grabbed the wrappers on the table, anchoring them to keep them from blowing away.

"Thing is," Jim continued. "Kerry Noland is always looking out for Kerry Noland. If I, or if you, can do anything to make her look good, she just might give you her support."

"Thanks. I'll keep that in mind."

"I'm gonna try to appeal to that side of her this afternoon. I'm trying to get some funds for the Charlotte Shelter."

The old guy wrote a phone number down on a napkin and left it under Todd's drink. "Call me if you need anything, okay?"

Todd nodded, picked up the napkin, and stuffed it into his shirt pocket.

Jim stood. "You'd better get back to work, and I better go find the boss-lady," he said, grinning.

Todd forced himself to smile.

The two walked through the back door and parted ways. Jim called back, "I'll see you at the shelter, Todd."

Todd waved and turned toward the I.T. offices. *Weird*.

. . .

She was about Emma's age and pretty, very pretty, laying on the examination bed in the trauma room. But her beauty was overshadowed by fear — the foreign surroundings, the pain of her injury, and the uncertain future. A thick neck brace, velcroed into place at the equestrian center by EMT personnel made the rest of her stylish clothes — the riding top, the jodhpurs, the calf-length black boots — seem foreign. A woman Angela took to be her mother stood a few feet away, near the closed door with eyes full of fear.

"What are you doing?" the girl exclaimed when a nurse sliced her blouse open with medical scissors.

"We need to determine the extent of your injuries," the doctor said. "You might have a broken clavicle but we want to see if there is any other trauma."

"Do you have to... ?"

"It's all right, dear," the mother, who had crossed her arms over her chest said.

"Tell us what happened," the doctor said behind his mask.

The woman spoke in a shaky voice. "We were at riding lessons... Every Tuesday... We've been going there for years." She seemed to have difficulty forming her words. Angela had seen it many times before. "Her horse... Beau... er, Beauregard... rose up and she fell off the back. She landed on her head... and her shoulders."

As the girl's top separated over her stomach, the woman stepped closer, eyes narrowed into a focused stare. "What are those?" Several straight lines sliced across her stomach, just below her navel. "Did that happen when she fell?"

The girl tried to cover the area with her hands but a nurse pulled them apart.

Angela peered closer. They looked suspiciously like cuts — made with a knife, razor, even scissors. Angela watched the girl's mother. Her eyes stared with incredulous intensity at the girl's midriff.

The nursing journals, classes, and seminars had warned of such marks — they could be signs of self-harm. Sometimes, the severely depressed cut themselves and these thin, parallel lines could be the result of such cuts. A thought pricked her mind, but she pushed it down. In a trauma seminar at a recent conference, a researcher said some people self-harm because it soothes them — makes them feel something other than the pain of sadness. The pinprick of a thought threatened to rise into consciousness, again. The marks on the girl's stomach — the stripes — sounded a lot like those on Emma's arms. Could Emma do something like that to herself?

The researcher had added that trauma victims who exhibited such traits often suffered from PTSD, tragic breakups, despair, extraordinary financial loss, physical or sexual abuse... Angela's underarms felt clammy. Her face flushed. *Why did she always seem depressed after visiting her Ex's house?*

She stopped herself, but her shoulders pressed down like a lead weight. Her chest was a tightening vise. The room seemed to swirl. "I need a minute," she whispered to a nurse standing nearby. The others in the room seemed to have the situation well under control.

"Are you all right?"

Angela nodded. Steadying herself against the wall, she headed across the hall to the break room. Holding the paper cup in both hands, she gulped down cool water.

But her thoughts simmered just below the surface. *I will kill the goddamn bastard.*

. . .

Kerry returned from her business leaders' luncheon, feeling good. Those monthly meetings were always full of bottom-feeding vendors, consultants, tech salesmen, and hiring firms, all fighting to snag a little of Bell's business. One by one they made their personal pitch to her, promising the best, the strongest, the leader-in-class solutions to propel Bell into the future. She toyed with each one — it was fun — and left the meeting with a handful of elegant business cards, which she dumped into the trash receptacle beside the elevator. She rose to the executive floor and slipped into her office through her private entrance before her first afternoon appointment. The entire morning, she had been annoyed by thoughts about the kid in programming. To her, he was a constant reminder of the bicycle incident. Every time she saw him — it seemed she'd run into him much more often recently — every time she heard his name, she imagined that rainy night and the idiot who rode his bike through the red light and into her path, but she had to move on. Todd didn't really matter. He was absent or tardy every other day. He did shoddy work. The guy was worthless.

Like her father.

As she reapplied red lipstick, her assistant peered through the doorway to let her know the Director of I.T. was there for her one o'clock. Then she added, "There's also a man who has been waiting almost an hour. He says he knows you."

Kerry waved her off, distracted. Her priority was to take care of her I.T. problem and relieve the frustration that had been bubbling up inside for months.

She began her conversation with Ronnie Davies by reiterating how important the I.T. department was at Bell. It was the supporting foundation by which other branches of the company could run. It had the potential to be one of the strategic advantages that would set them apart from their competition. She poured on the accolades, gearing up for the kill. She said I.T. wasn't reaching its best-in-class potential because some of the programmers weren't performing as well as they should.

"Davies, it's time to clean house — time to remove the low performers." She stared directly into his eyes. "Specifically, Todd Sanders."

He was stunned. His eyes widened and his face paled. "Are you sure? He's been through a real tough time, lately. He will bounce back and things will get better."

"He is holding your department back, right?"

"Well, just a bit right now, but..."

"We can't have that. We have too much work to do. I'd like to bring on another call center next year and I can't do it if he's burdening your entire team and the company."

"I know he's been off his game, lately..."

She slapped her desk for emphasis. "This isn't a game and we are not playing around."

Davies was silent.

When wimps like Davies shut up, she'd won, and she always won. "Do it this week, or I'll find someone who will."

He mumbled agreement and walked out the door as her assistant slipped back inside. "The other gentleman is still here. His name is Jim Bishop."

"Bishop?" *Son of a... What does he want?* "You know I don't have time to see everyone who wanders into the office. Get rid..." She peered around her assistant. The tall man, dressed in a stylish but outdated business suit, stood in the doorway. Their eyes met and she knew she couldn't blow him off. He smiled and waved. He always had a charming smile. Much nicer than the others.

"Invite him in." She painted a smile on her face.

Jim Bishop extended his hand and she accepted it. "Jim! How nice to see you." Leaning in, she air-kissed his cheek. She motioned to a chair and returned to her place behind her desk. "How are you?" she asked, hands clasped together before her. She played the hostess game as well as anybody.

"I'm all right. Fine." He appeared relaxed, but his right foot bounced like a jackhammer. She remembered that nervous tic of his when they shared dinner on road trips, just a few years ago. Nervousness was a sign of weakness — the man was afraid of her.

"What was it I heard? Your wife..." She was unsure of what had happened and how to turn her words into condolences. Not that she cared about either.

His foot stopped bouncing. "Yes. Jean passed away a few months ago." His right hand rubbed the ring on his left.

"Oh. I'm so sorry for your loss." The words leaked out without thought or emotion. She might as easily have said, "How are you?" or "Take care," or "Screw you." Still feeling a rush from the business luncheon and demanding Davies fire his programmer, she thirsted for more blood. Leaning forward, she offered her most sincere expression and a glimpse of her best features. "How can I help you, Jimmy?" It would be fun to play cat and mouse again. She wondered if Jim might be interested in restarting their friendship now that his wife was out of the way.

He cleared his throat. "First, thank you for taking time to see me. I know how busy you are."

She detected a faint stutter of nervousness in his voice.

"I hear great things about Bell. You must be doing a wonderful job."

"We work hard. You know how it is. You and I worked very hard to make Bell what it is today. We had some good times together." She licked the red lipstick that coated her lips.

Jim hesitated, then nodded. "I recently volunteered at a homeless shelter near the Fourth Ward. I've helped them several nights over the past couple of weeks. They're a good outfit. They provide a place to sleep and breakfast and dinner for about a hundred people each night.... more when it's really cold."

Penance for something in the past? She kept smiling but said nothing. She remembered Jim as one of the stronger men she had broken. It took time, but eventually she'd lured him into a bedroom in a W Hotel in New York, or Chicago, or Dallas, and made him hers. But the purpose of this visit wasn't to ask for a date. He just wanted money and she wasn't about to give any.

"I was wondering if Bell might be willing to sponsor the shelter. If you could donate just a few thousand a year, it would really help."

Rage bubbled up inside of her, threatening to explode, but she tamped it down. "You know, I get so many people in here begging for money. I can't support every charity request that comes across my desk."

Jim leaned forward. "I know, Kerry, but this shelter does a really good job. I know when I worked for you, we were very concerned about how the public perceived Bell, and giving to the shelter..."

She couldn't hold back. "You son of a bitch." She placed both hands on her desk, like a cat ready to pounce. "I'm not the Federal Reserve. Why should I give you anything? You screwed me and now you're asking for payback?"

"No, it's nothing like that..." Jim mumbled.

"You didn't even have the balls to break it off to my face. I got a call from my COO while I'm vacationing in Southeast Asia, saying you quit."

"I had to get out. It was ruining my marriage." His head nodded back and forth as he searched the carpet.

"I never gave a damn about your marriage."

"Obviously."

"If you were so worried about your goddam marriage, why did you take me to bed? Sounds like your wife wasn't taking care of you. Not much of a marriage, was it?" Her voice was rising. Her secretary, concern painting her face, closed the office door.

"I didn't 'take you to bed'," Jim countered. "You're the one who seduced me... like you seduced other men in this organization. That's what you do, Kerry. You lure men to bed because it gives you power. And you thrive on that. You need that."

"I don't need anything," she said and rose from her chair. "You're the needy one. You're here to beg for money. And when you worked for me, you needed me."

"What we did... was just a bad mistake."

"Mistake? I am not a mistake!" The room was getting warmer.

"We never should have..."

"But we did, and you enjoyed it!"

Jim lowered his head and stared at the floor. "I made a terrible mistake. Jean was so much better than me. She never let go."

"Then go ask her to fund your damn shelter," Kerry shouted. "Get out of my office."

Beside the office door she had just opened, her assistant appeared worried. Jim remained standing, staring. "All this... All of this is going to come crashing down around you one day and you will be left alone. When that happens, remember the good people in this world... the saints... 'cause they're the ones you left and they will be the only ones that can save you." He turned as one on a mission and walked through the door.

"If he comes back," Kerry said to her assistant, "call Security."

"Yes, ma'am."

• • •

Weird. The talk with the old man, Jim Whatever-his-name, seemed creepy. It was odd that they had bumped into each other. Todd wondered if the old guy was following him.

He left early. He just didn't feel like working. If anybody asked, he could tell them he had to do community service. He drove north, past Uptown where new apartment buildings were rising from the asphalt like stalagmites in a cave. Somebody he met in church had just moved into one. He'd said a studio apartment cost more than the gross salary of a minimum wage job. His apartment sported amenities like a private rooftop bar, dog walkers, and an in-house masseuse. The view, he said, was priceless.

Todd would never be able to live there, even if he left Bell. After all, his coding skills, which he once thought were excellent, really weren't that great and he'd never be able to afford to go back to school to improve them. He surely couldn't afford an uptown apartment on a pauper's salary and was doomed to peasantry, living in places worse off than the Weasley's burrow in Harry Potter. He'd never get a high paying job, not with his spotty record. He'd have to explain the bike incident to potential employers. It would stay with him like the scent of a dying corpse... "I killed a man..."

He passed through the Fourth Ward and pulled over beside a large, old cemetery. Compelled to explore, desperate to clear his head, he got out of his car. Dirt-gray headstones were lined up in some places like rows of soldiers and strewn about in others like foundations of abandoned buildings. Wide open areas presented opportunities for more headstones in the future. *Death never dies.*

Todd walked along pathways and read the names on the markers. One told of a Civil War soldier. Another simply said, "Daddy." There were several Smiths, and Jones, and Browns. Todd chuckled at one which said only, "Has Bean" in large letters. *No spellcheck for gravestones.*

The graveyard behind him was filled not only with dead people, but dead hopes and dreams. Why celebrate the dead with elaborate memorials when each and every one of them had ultimately failed? No matter what their lives were like — business executive or homeless bum — all ended here. He'd end here too, one day. Maybe sooner than later.

As he returned to his car, he noticed a light-colored sedan parked across the street. He couldn't make out the figure inside, but as he walked toward the road, the driver started the car and drove away. The car seemed familiar, like one he'd seen at Bell, or *Living Waters*, or perhaps his apartment complex.

His drive home took an eternity.

CHAPTER SEVEN

Jim needed help. Feeling humiliated, owned, and verbally assaulted, he longed for redemption. Jean had forgiven him, but could he forgive himself?

He was sitting in a small diner around the corner from his home, eating a Reuben and feeling a bit sorry for himself. The restaurant was a throw-back to the old greasy spoons of the past. High round stools lined the counter across from a window to the kitchen. Chrome fixtures adorned the place — the overhead fans, table edges, chairs, booths. The diner was half silver.

He was thinking the place could use a makeover with blond wood, recessed lighting, and maybe brown backs on the chairs when Rev. Allen Rhodes, head hanging low, feet shuffling as if they bore a weighty load on an exhausted frame, approached the silver-edged counter and chose a seat on a red-backed swivel chair. The waitress leaned in and spoke to him in a soft voice. Allen seemed to know her — he probably came here for lunch often. With a brief smile and a nod, he accepted the plain white cup and saucer and stirred some cream into the black liquid.

The act reminded Jim of his father, sitting at the kitchen table in the late sixties, stirring his coffee and trying to understand the Vietnam war, the riots, and the changes the nation faced in such a tumultuous time. He wasn't wealthy or well-educated, but he had tried to comprehend those things that were new and different. At the top of his worry list was his youngest son, David. A smart kid with good elementary school grades, he was also somewhat of a recluse, choosing to be by himself instead of with other boys his age. It was not unusual to find David building a complicated plastic model all Saturday morning and afternoon instead of playing football or baseball with Jim and his friends. Try as he might, Jim's dad could not coax David to be more outgoing. David just wasn't like him or Jim.

The image in the diner was disconcerting. Why did this minister, a so-called man of God, seem so troubled, so perplexed? *What was on his mind? Who do ministers talk to when they are down? Who ministers to the minister?* Allen's BLT was delivered by the waitress with a smile, but he didn't seem to notice either. She walked away, and the sandwich remained untouched.

As if struggling with a competitive chess match dilemma, Jim contemplated his next move. Should he go sit on the empty stool next to Rev. Rhodes? It wasn't in his nature to offer a sympathetic ear. He preferred to keep his social relationships fairly shallow. A pat on the back? Sure. A conversation with a shrink in a counselor's office? Uh, uh. He wouldn't know what to say. Introspective navel-gazing was not his strength. He might embarrass himself... or worse, his friend. Even so, he was concerned.

Picking up the plate containing the remainder of his Reuben and a small pile of ridged potato chips, he approached the counter. "Rev. Rhodes?" His own voice sounded timid.

Allen didn't seem to hear him.

Jim tried again. "Hi. Rev. Rhodes?"

As Allen's head turned, his eyes, almost covered by drooping eyelids, met Jim's. In an instant his countenance shifted, a smile filled his face, and his shoulders rose. "Hi, Jim," he said. But a trace of pretense lingered.

"I saw you having lunch... wondered if I could join you. That is, if you're not busy."

Allen shifted into professional minister mode. "Of course. Please."

Jim sat next to him and Allen picked up his sandwich and took a small bite. "Isn't this a beautiful day? Looks like things might be warming up," Jim offered, feeling like he'd just said nothing.

"Yes, it is gorgeous outside."

"So how are things going at the church?" Jim asked.

"Good. How are you doing these days?" Allen asked.

"I'm doing good. Better every day." Their conversation was empty. Distance, an enormous chasm, separated them. Jim had no idea how to bridge the gap, but it occurred to him that if he shared his own burden, perhaps Allen would reciprocate. So he put his head down and just blundered into it. "Actually, it hasn't been that great lately."

Allen tilted his head, encouraging Jim to continue.

"I just got reamed out by a woman... to be totally honest, someone I had a fling with while I was still married to Jean. I cheated. I hurt Jean. I've always regretted it."

"How did Jean take it?"

"She was mad, at first. Real mad."

"I would guess so."

"But she came around, we worked through it and moved on." He felt like a kid admitting to his teacher he had cheated on his test.

"Now that sounds like the Jean I knew. She was very strong."

Jim shook his head and fought back the tears he always felt when thinking about the affair with Kerry Noland.

"I'm sure Jean let it go," Allen said. "You probably should, too." He took a larger bite of his sandwich.

While Jim felt better, he wasn't through. "Allen, can I ask you a question?"

"Of course."

"Are you okay? Is something bothering you?"

Allen shifted his sandwich plate to the side and wiped his lips with a paper napkin. "No. I'm fine. Just a little tired."

Jim forced himself to remain still. He felt uneasy, but a voice inside told him to stay with it.

Allen looked in his direction out of the corner of his eye. "I'm okay. Really. Just some personal stuff."

Jim barreled ahead. "Allen, I'm green. I don't know a lot, but I can listen... if you want to talk."

Allen said nothing.

"Trust me... Allen." The hair on the back of his neck felt moist. "Well, if you ever need..."

"Ok," Allen said before Jim could go further. He sipped his coffee. "Things are rough at the church. Some of the members complain. A lot. Since everybody puts something in the offering plate, everybody feels like they pay my salary, and everybody has an opinion."

"I had no idea..." The floodgates opened.

Allen turned to face the kitchen window behind the counter. He took a deep breath. "Some people think I spend too much time at the homeless shelter, or at the forum on gun violence, or on the spouse abuse board. They want me to spend more time on my sermons. I guess they want somebody who's a better preacher. They're threatening to leave the church for that *Living Waters* church. Some have already left."

Jim had to bite his tongue to keep from mentioning that preaching wasn't one of Allen's strongest suits.

"The church is struggling to pay its budget. Some of the folks who left were big donors, and it's not easy to make up the difference."

Jim made a mental note to put more in the offering plate. "I never thought about it that way. I always worked for corporations. If we went through hard times, we just cut costs... usually heads."

"Doesn't really work that way in the nonprofit world. When you cut costs, you cut programs and people stop being involved... or worse, they get pissed and go somewhere else."

Jim wanted to say something but came up with nothing.

Allen turned to face him. "To tell you the truth, the biggest thing on my mind right now is my son. He's a junior in high school, and I worry about the influence some of his friends have on him."

Jim knew nothing about kids and his mind was blank.

Allen waved his hand. "It's okay. I didn't sleep well last night and I guess I'm kind of tired." His eyes met Jim's. "Thank you."

Jim was about to offer a glib, "You're welcome," when Allen checked his watch, stood, placed some money on the counter, and called to the waitress, "Thanks, Ella Jean." He turned back to Jim. "I do appreciate your concern." He placed a firm hand on Jim's shoulder. "I hate to run, but I have a staff meeting in about fifteen minutes." With that he hustled out of the diner.

Jim pushed back the plate containing what little remained of his sandwich. The waitress leaned over and withdrew the plate.

"Thank you," Jim mumbled. Somehow, his shoulders felt lighter.

Ella Jean winked and smiled and turned back to the kitchen window.

Another cold night in Charlotte. Sheryl hugged the flimsy clothes around her to keep her baby warm as the line crept along the sidewalk. She had arrived later than usual because she had fallen asleep in the library and now she was at the end of the women's line. She needed to get into the building... for her baby.

She neared the doorway as a woman holding a clipboard said the shelter was full — no room for any more women. People grumbled, but the woman shook her head. She handed out slips of paper — names and addresses of other shelters that might have vacancies. Sheryl did not protest. She turned back to the street to search for a warm place.

"Sheryl," a voice called. "Sheryl!" She turned her head toward the voice and the woman in the doorway called again, "Come here."

Sheryl hung her head low as she walked away. When someone called on a street person, it was usually kinda bad. It was better to stay out of their way.

The volunteer ran down the steps. She was out of breath when she caught up to Sheryl. "I need to talk with you."

Sheryl turned again to walk across the street this time worried that the woman might be trapping her — to get her baby. The woman touched her arm. "We have room for you," she said.

Sheryl looked up into the woman's face wondering if this was a trick or if it was real.

The woman smiled and nodded. "Come with me."

Hooded head down, Sheryl followed through the doorway into the shelter. People who had been turned away stared. It was crowded inside. The woman took Sheryl back to a place off to one side where an air mattress had been set up for the night.

"You can sleep here. I wish we had a more comfortable mattress, but we set this up at the last minute for you."

Sheryl turned the door... for a way to escape, if necessary. It was always smart to know where the exits were.

"It's all right, Sheryl. You'll be okay here," the woman said, and there was a genuine kindness in her voice. "Please make yourself comfortable." She walked back toward the kitchen to help prepare the evening meal.

As Sheryl laid out her meager belongings, the shelter director squatted beside her. He was a small msn, short and slim. "Sheryl. I'm so glad you came back tonight."

Lowering her head, she stared at the blanket on the mattress. She didn't like to be singled out. It was safer with the group. And she didn't like being singled out by men.

"Do you remember Mr. Jim? He's a volunteer. You talked with him a few days ago."

Sheryl stared at the floor.

"He called earlier and said he had made arrangements at a clinic to give you care before you have your baby."

She shook her head. "No. They'll take my baby."

"No, they won't, Sheryl. I promise. They will make sure you and the baby are healthy. They want to help you with your baby."

She shook her head. "Costs too much."

"There's no fee. It will be free." He handed her a slip of paper containing a street address. "Go there as soon as you can. They will take care of you."

There was a phone number at the bottom of the piece of paper. "Jim?"

"Yes. He said to call him if you need a ride."

She searched the man's eyes, sensing she could trust him. When he walked away, she stuffed the piece of paper into her tote bag. Maybe...

. . .

"Hey, Preach!"

Allen, deep in thought about Paul's apparent mix-up with white supremacists, heard the call and raised his head. A short, skinny man with a disheveled goatee followed behind him. Allen had parked his car in the empty church parking lot — it was always empty during the weekdays, and half-empty Sundays — on his way to his office. "How can I help you?"

The little runt of a man caught up with Allen. "I just wanted to ask you a question." He wore a short-sleeved shirt. A tattoo of an American flag hanging from a rifle peeked out beneath one sleeve. Allen thought he must have been chilly, wearing short sleeves in February. He was late, so he tried to leap-frog over the small talk to get to what he thought was the real issue. "If you need a place to stay and a hot meal, we support the Charlotte Shelter off Tryon."

"No, it ain't nothin' like that."

"Okay…"

The old guy nodded toward the church building. "Would you say your church has a lot of family folk here?"

"Oh, yes. We are blessed with many families."

"White families? Black families?"

"Yes. White families. We need to reach out to more of our black families, though."

The old man scratched his beard. "Hmmm."

"Is there something on your mind?"

Their eyes met and the old man nodded and said, "Family is important."

"I couldn't agree with you more." Allen started to say goodbye.

"How 'bout your family, Preach?"

Allen froze. No one ever asked about a minister's family. They always assumed it was healthy. *Unless…* He scanned his memory, searching for a way the old geezer might know of his trouble with his son. "Why do you ask?"

"Family is important," Gene answered again and nodded again.

"What did you say your name was?" Allen asked.

"My name is Eugene, but you can call me Gene."

"Well, Gene, my family is about like every family. We have good times and we have some tough times now and then. I'd like to think the good far outweighs the bad."

That seemed to satisfy the old man. He nodded his head. "That's good. Family is important," he said a third time.

The two men stood stock still, each waiting for the other to speak. Finally, Gene broke the silence and said, "I'd better be moving on, I guess. You take care, Preach."

"You, too," Allen said. "God bless you."

"And take care of Paul," Gene called. He hummed as he walked down the street. Allen recognized the song, "It's A Family Affair," by Sly and the Family Stone.

Community service kept him pretty busy after work, and Todd welcomed the activity. On most nights when he wasn't at the homeless shelter, he served at the *Living Waters* church where he was upgrading the organization's multi-media system. He worked alone, switching out the older cables with newer ones and adding several more mic input jacks for greater flexibility during worship services. After a couple of hours at the church, he would return home to spend another hour or two troubleshooting the church's website.

Since the accident, Todd had stayed pretty much to himself. Everything had changed. His former fiancé, Mandy, was a fading memory. He had little time for his other friends — the few that he had. Most of them had other groups, other activities, and his life was consumed with *Living Waters*.

But now relationships with his peers at *Living Waters* were waning. He had emailed his resume to Carley at Red Ventures, but she hadn't gotten back to him. He supposed she must be busy. Steve had been distant as well, focused on his online monitoring project during work and disappearing when everyone went home.

As Todd made his way into the church sanctuary to work on the rewiring project he passed Steve Thurmond's SUV in the parking lot. So this was where he went after work. He made an abrupt left turn up the sidewalk to the education wing and entered through a side door. Halfway down the hall, light from one of the classrooms bounced off the gleaming linoleum floor; someone was using that room. He glanced inside and saw a small group of church members sitting on metal folding chairs in a tight huddle. On one side of the circle, Steve Thurmond leaned in, arms on his knees, listening intently. Curious, Todd stopped in the hallway past the door and listened to the conversation. One of the associate ministers was leading some sort of an outreach strategy group. One by one, they were talking about new church members. He mentioned each by name. Others in the group would offer insight on how each person was assimilating.

A sense of unease filled his gut and he turned up the hallway toward the sanctuary. That's when he heard his name.

"What about Todd Sanders. How's he doing?"

"I think he's settling in," Steve said.

"Is he involved?"

"He's helping out the multi-media team — doing some upgrades here and there."

"And fellowship?"

"He was playing volleyball with our singles group but his community service commitments have kept him from it recently. Maybe he'll start again after he's gotten his hours in."

"We'll pray that he'll come back to the volleyball team then," the minister said. "But it sounds like he's found a place here at *Living Waters*. Praise God." Squinting through a crack between the door and the wall, Todd saw Steve sitting back in his chair, gloating.

"And what about Crystal Robertson?" the minister continued. "She's that new member who joined a couple of weeks ago. She works at... She teaches at the community college."

"Ah, yes. She could be a strong influence on her students," someone out of Todd's sight said.

"And she's going through a divorce. Apparently, her ex is a doctor. He had an affair with one of his patients and now they're getting married. I heard Crystal tell someone she has a solid pre-nupt and expects to make the most of it."

Todd wiped a hand across his forehead. It was damp.

"Crystal could be a vital member of our congregation. Steve, help her become more involved here, okay?"

"Sure. And what about Todd?"

"We'll continue to pray for him, but it sounds like he's doing fine. Besides, he may not have anywhere else to go."

Todd's knees felt like they were made of balsa wood and ready to snap off. He leaned back against the concrete block wall and forced himself to breathe. Sounds of commotion indicated the meeting was breaking up. He pushed himself away from the wall and hurried up the hallway to the sanctuary.

• • •

On cold nights, the most vulnerable suffered the most. They filled the lobby of the Wesley Memorial Emergency Room, many suffering from flu and pneumonia.

This cold night was no exception.

Sometimes, Angela would watch them through the little glass window of the examination area door and wonder how they survived. The sick children were the worse. Fortunately, most of the time they had someplace to go — a family member's house, a neighbor's house — after visiting the hospital. Still, the adults could not be ignored and the lobby was full of them tonight.

Angela escorted her fifth patient into the examination room and checked his chart. "Eugene?"

"Yes, ma'am. Eugene Johnson." He coughed loud and long.

"How long have you had this cough?"

"I don't know. Several days." He sniffed phlegm up his nose and into the back of his throat. Dirt painted the joints of his fingers and the tips of his fingernails. He combed his long, scraggly beard with them.

She took his vitals and entered them into the nearby computer. "Do you have someplace to stay tonight?"

"No, ma'am. The shelters are all full."

"Do you have someone you can stay with... family... friend?"

He shook his head.

"You know you can't go out in this cold weather. You have walking pneumonia and that can kill you in these conditions."

"Yes, ma'am."

Angela wearied at the thought and the number of cases like his. Tonight, people would die without help. "Okay, Eugene. I'm going to give you an antibiotic shot and some medicine to help your cough. I'm not supposed to tell you this, but if you go back into the lobby, way over toward the quiet end, you can rest there for the night. Security won't disturb you." She sighed deeply.

"Thank you, ma'am." His eyes studied her name badge, "Ms. Griffen." While she prepped the shot, he added, "You seem a bit troubled tonight, ma'am."

Angela shook him off. "It's just a busy night."

"Ya sure that's all?"

She felt like the old guy was getting nosey. "Yes."

"Family?" he asked.

Angela snapped her head up from the checklist before her. "Of course. Doesn't everyone have family concerns?" He was irritating her.

He coughed another series of severe hacks, leaning over, holding his chest. Angela took advantage of the gap in his questions to ask, "Do you have any close relatives?"

"Nah," he said. "My ex is in South Carolina. Otherwise, nobody in particular."

"How long have you been on the street?" she asked, trying to stay ahead of his questions.

"Long time. Long time." He hacked again. "You know, family's important. Family's what got you here and family's what keeps you going and family's what sets you free in the end."

"But you just said you don't have any close family, Eugene. What keeps you going?"

"My family's out there," he said, nodding toward the lobby. "They're in the shelters and under the bridges. They're in the woods."

His answer seemed sad.

"You gotta look after your family... especially the little ones."

She wondered where he was going. It was as if he knew... sensed something about her. She decided to stay quiet. It was safer that way.

After administering the injection, she guided him to the door. "Now, take care of yourself, Eugene. Go get some rest in the lobby."

Eugene hacked again, leaning over and threatening to expel his guts. "You take care too, Missy. And take real good care of that daughter of yours."

She turned back inside and stopped in her tracks, her mouth agape. "What do you know about my daughter?"

Eugene stepped back. "Nothing. Just took a wild guess. But we do have to keep an eye out for our young 'uns. Dontchaknow?"

Another patient was in one of the examination rooms, so she entered and began the process of evaluating her.

When she returned to the lobby during her next break, Eugene was gone.

. . .

The call came in the early evening, just after Jim had finished dinner. He didn't like eating alone, but given his current situation, he had no one to eat with... except the nights he worked at the shelter and dined with the homeless guests.

He picked up the phone and was surprised to hear Allen's voice. "Jim," Allen said. "I wonder if you might be able to drop by the house tonight. I've got a favor to ask."

Bright lights welcomed Jim through the open garage door when he arrived at Allen's house. Allen was inside wearing a sweaty purple Seventy-Sixers jersey and clashing bright red shorts, holding a classic boxer stance, and pounding a large Everlast punching bag that hung from the rafters. His athletic body dipped and bowed to the bag as if it were a real fighter. Allen waved, unlaced the strings of his boxing gloves, and dropped them to a bench in the back of the garage. They met on the driveway and shook hands.

"I forgot you used to box. Didn't know you still did."

"Picked it up when I lived in Atlanta as a kid. It keeps me in shape and helps me work off stress these days. You should try it."

Jim noticed something in Allen's voice, almost imperceptible through the small talk... a shakiness, a higher pitch, something. "I'm glad you came over," he said, taking a seat on a nearby weight lifting bench. Jim leaned against the side of the Honda opposite him and stuffed his hands into his pockets.

"Jim, I have a huge favor."

Seldom had anyone spoken those words to him. Maybe once when an employee needed some extra time off to care for a loved one, or when his brother needed a loan, but that was about it. "Sure, Allen. Anything." He leaned forward.

Allen reached behind himself into an old duffel bag, extracted a paper sack, and handed it to Jim as if it contained a venomous snake. "I don't know of anyone else I could ask to do this. No one else I know would understand." The bag trembled in his hand. "I need you to get rid of this... safely and discreetly. If you turn it in to the police, make sure no one knows I gave it to you."

Jim nodded and took the sack from him, feeling like a spy taking a secret doomsday device from another spy. It was heavy. He opened the bag to see the pistol lying in the bottom. "Jesus..."

"Yeah. Jesus."

He closed the bag and looked up, "What's this all about, Allen?"

Allen stared into his face as if measuring whether he could trust him with this task. "I got it from... a relative, but that's all I can say. The less you know, the better."

Jim flinched, felt his eyes twitch a bit and studied the bag again. "Why me? Certainly anyone else..."

"I'm not sure... I don't know... I think I can trust you. Most of the other people around here couldn't keep a secret if God Himself told them to. I'm afraid anyone who's been in our church for awhile might go ballistic. My neighbors would be even worse. You seem reliable, haven't been in the church that long, and you said to contact you if I needed anything..."

"Well, I don't know who I'd talk to about this, anyway."

"Thank you, Jim. You're a life saver."

"Never thought of myself that way."

"Well, you are."

Fear tainted an odd combination of gratitude and confusion as he placed the bag on the back seat of his car and drove away.

⁕ ⁕ ⁕

"Emma," Angela said through cotton-dry lips. "How's softball going?"

"Fine."

"Are you enjoying it?"

A shrug. "Sure. We're five and two this season."

Angela frowned. "But is it fun?"

The two sat at the kitchen table after dinner. Angela had swapped hours with another nurse to come home early. Until that moment, Emma had seemed preoccupied. When Angela asked the question, her body stiffened like concrete. She reached for her soft drink — an unusual treat for a school night, hesitated in midair, and then pulled her hand back into her lap.

"You always seem so down when you come home from your father's. It just doesn't seem like you have much fun."

Nothing.

"You never talk about your games."

A shrug. She rubbed her finger lightly across the cover of her Biology textbook.

"Do you not like visitations with your father?"

"I don't know. They're okay."

"Does he do anything that bothers you?"

Nothing.

"You know, visiting people you don't like... making you watch TV shows you don't care about... forcing you to go places you don't want to go... ?"

Emma slowly bit her lower lip. "Uh, no."

Angela ground her teeth. "I noticed some scratches on your forearm."

They weren't showing, but Emma tugged her shirt sleeves down farther.

"Emma, talk to me."

"Mom, leave me alone. Nothing's wrong. Stop bothering me." She stood to leave.

"Sit down," Angela said, shocked by the sternness in her own voice.

Scolded, her daughter sat back in her chair.

"Honey, I love you. We had a girl in the ER the other day who had similar cuts. We think she was abused by someone, so I've been concerned about you."

Her head hung low, but Angela could still see her eyes growing moist.

"Show me your arm, sweetie," Angela said, reaching out both hands.

Emma stretched across the table. Angela drew back her sleeve and placed Emma's hand in her own. The scratches were worse than she had expected. Single, parallel lines traced a track toward her wrists.

Angela breathed out slowly, doing all she could to stay calm. The walls in their tiny kitchen seemed to close in. "Emma. Have you been cutting yourself?"

Tears poured down the girl's red cheeks. Without speaking, she nodded.

Angela shook. The worst thing she could imagine was happening. With all her strength, she made herself stay seated, stay objective, stay patient... at least for the moment. She slid her left hand over the cuts on Emma's right arm, trying somehow to hide them, trying somehow to heal them. "Your father?"

Emma pulled back her hands, dashed around the table, and collapsed into her mother's waiting arms. Sobs like Angela had seldom heard exploded from deep inside. She rocked her daughter as she had when she was born, and when she was two, and when she was five.

"I hate softball. I hate it there." She sniffed. "He makes fun of me. He pushes me... hard. He scares me, Mom. He calls me names."

Angela knew such humiliation was some sick way of getting back at her. "He doesn't mean that, honey."

"Yes, he does. I hate him."

"Don't say that."

"I do. Daddy gets mad a lot, especially when I make mistakes on the field. When he's mad, he hits me."

Angela paused. This was something different. She never thought Evan would be violent.

Without saying a word, Emma rolled the sleeve on her arm up above the red scratch marks. A bruise, a dark purple halo surrounding a red and yellow center, stood out like a shooting target. "When I struck out, he made me do extra batting practice while he pitched. He hit me on purpose. A lot." Angela slid her hand up to the spot just shy of touching it.

"He also slaps me when he gets really mad. Slaps don't usually cause bruises. He calls me names in front of my friends." Emma rolled up the other sweatshirt sleeve to reveal a row of four orange smudge-like impressions where someone had grasped her forearm hard. "After we lost."

Emma twisted her torso and tugged up the sweatshirt to reveal additional bruises just below her ribs on her back. "More batting practice." Angela knew about Evan's eighty mph fastballs from his high school baseball games.

Angela took Emma's chin in her hand and turned her face so their eyes met. "I am so sorry, Emma." She felt in her heart — feared in her soul there was more. "Has he done anything else? I need to know."

"No."

Swallowing deeply, Angela pressed on.

"Has he touched you where he shouldn't?"

Ridges on her nose showed the thought repulsed Emma. Then, a whisper, "no."

"Are you sure?"

Emma's head nodded.

Angela longed to trust her daughter completely, but she had no trust for Evan. She searched Emma's eyes for an eternity and then pulled her into her own arms for a strong, protective hug. Torn between fear that Emma wasn't telling everything and gratitude that Evan's abuse was not sexual, Angela held on to her daughter and held onto the moment as long as she could. But she also knew physical and emotional abuse could be just as devastating for a young girl as sexual abuse.

"Mom, what are you going to do?"

"We need help. We need to find someone we can talk with about this... to learn how to handle it best. And then we need to learn how to deal with your father. You won't have to go to his house ever again."

"I don't want to get into trouble."

"You've done nothing wrong, Sweetie. You won't get into trouble."

She would reserve trouble for the one who deserved it.

CHAPTER EIGHT

Jim ran into Peggy Crutchfield, her grandson Mike, and of course Jackson Browne, at Independence Park several times. The last time, Jim brought a radio-controlled speedboat, which he gave to Mike to race in the lake. The boy steered the craft across the silky pond for about thirty minutes before it ran through a gaggle of geese and their chicks, pissing off their mothers. Peggy insisted they take a break, so Jim helped Mike put the racing boat into dry dock.

The time with Mike and Peggy was a welcome respite from the loneliness of Jim's home. He enjoyed the light conversation with a new friend and the wild antics of a boy and his dog in the cool winter afternoons. Each time, Peggy brought snacks — brownies, cookies, and something made of cheese and dough and bits of sausage that Jim had never eaten before. Most of the snacks were delicious.

"Isn't this heavenly?" Peggy sighed late one afternoon as the sun was threatening to disappear below the Charlotte skyline. They were walking on the trail beside Little Sugar Creek, which ran along the perimeter of the park. "I wish my husband would have visited this park with me. I think he would have liked it."

Jim wished he had come to the park with Jean so they could've shared the sights and sounds of this beautiful oasis. But that was in the past and Jim was coming to grips with the life ahead of him, and his need to take advantage of every enjoyable moment.

"You know, he and I used to go to a little Italian restaurant just up the road. They had the most delicious pasta dishes, and desert to die for."

An invitation to dinner? Jim wasn't ready to bite. "Say, do you ever see Ms. Griffen at the hospital?"

"Nurse Griffen? Oh, yes. Quite often. She always seems so busy, running here and there frantically, like a cat with her tail on fire."

"Well, the emergency room is a busy place."

"Perhaps. It seems like she's always poking her nose into everything going on around her. I think she has her hands full, raising a daughter as a single parent and working full time." A determined frown crossed her brow.

He recalled Angela's kindness and concern when Jean had passed and when he was attacked while trying to give away blankets to the poor. "I'm just glad she was there when I needed support."

Peggy was quiet for a few moments. "If you ever need support, you can always call me." The come-on tainted the tone of her words.

Jim looked to the setting sun. "I've got volunteer service at the homeless shelter tonight. I should head back."

Peggy seemed to take his words as a rejection. They corralled Mike and Jackson Browne and went their separate ways.

Jim picked up his pace on his walk home. If he hurried he could catch the tip-off of the Hornets and the Heat game on TV. He didn't have anything else important to do that evening.

The numbers and letters bouncing on the screen in a hypnotic language-dance mesmerized Todd. He could have stared at them for hours. So, he did. He was startled when Ron Davies invited him into his office.

Todd took a seat in the cloth-covered chair in front of the director's desk and stared at the director's coffee mug bearing the words, "Give me DOS or give me Death." Davies sat behind his desk and his voice took on a business-like monotone style. "Todd, as you know, we have a very competitive office environment. We want to attract the most motivated system engineers we can, and that requires everyone to be at the top of his or her game," he said, steepling his fingers.

Todd had heard his comment before — work at Bell was not a game. He closed his eyes, sure of what was coming next.

"I'm being forced to make some changes. Your work has not been up to par, lately. I'm getting pressure from management to improve our output, so we're going to, uh, that is, we're going to encourage you to pursue other career opportunities."

"Huh?"

Davies took a drink from the coffee mug, grimaced, and said, "Todd, I know you've had a rough time over the last six or eight months, and we've tried to be flexible, but we have to release you."

Todd stared back without emotion. He had known this day would come. Better sooner than later. After all, he deserved it. He was a royal screw-up.

Davies slid a folder across the desk. "We've put together a severance package, quite a fair one, I must say, to help you transition."

Todd stared at it like it was a pile of crap.

"You'll find we are giving you a week of outplacement services — these guys can help you write your resume and can let you use their library of business interests in the area."

Todd stared at him. "Business interests?"

"You know, other companies you might want to consider... er... sending your CV to." Trickles of sweat stained Davies' collar. "In addition, we're giving you a week of pay for each year you've worked at Bell. That's three weeks of pay, without benefits, of course, and I've been able to talk our compensation department to give you one additional week of pay." He waited for a response. "So you'll have a month's income while you search for another job."

Todd wondered if Davies wanted thanks.

"Do you have any questions?"

Todd shook his head.

"Ok," Davies said, offering his hand.

Todd reached forward and placed his limp hand into his former Director's. Turning, he walked through the office, down the aisle, and out the door without looking back. He didn't care about collecting his belongs from his desk. Nothing had any value, except his small statue of Gandolf, but that no longer mattered.

David was becoming a royal pain. Since Jean had passed, he had made it his job to keep tabs on his brother. He called him once a week — every Sunday at 4:00 in the afternoon. Exactly 4:00. They usually didn't talk about much — news, weather, movies they'd seen on television — but they talked every week, none the less. He also visited once every month. Jim tried to talk him out of it — airplane flights were expensive and David couldn't keep it up forever, but he ignored his comments.

Jim was getting tired of sitting in the living room, drinking bottles of Coors Light, and watching sports. He felt more like a host than a brother... A bad host.

On his most recent trip, after dinner at Olive Garden — they always ate at Olive Garden — they returned home to watch the Magic play the Hawks. David was loading the dishwasher with plates and glasses from Jim's sink — somehow, Jim let them pile up — when he pulled a brown paper sack from beneath the counter.

"What's this?" He walked through the kitchen door and showed the bag to Jim. "I was looking for soap."

"It's not takeout," Jim said, taking the bag and its dangerous contents from his brother. He breathed in and rubbed his forehead. "David, I'm glad you're here. Really. However, it's been over three months since Jean passed, and I'm fine."

"Of course you are, Jim. What's in the bag?"

Jim reached in and drew out the black pistol. "It's something I promised to dispose of... for a friend. I just have no idea how. I guess I'll take it to the Sherriff's office. I don't want to drop it in the trash 'cause somebody at the dump might find it and get hurt. I could throw it in the Catawba River, but that's too far to drive."

"Where'd you say you got it?"

"It's no big deal. Just a friend asked me to dispose of it, and I don't know how to do it."

David took the gun from Jim and said, "Damn." He inspected it, turning it over in his hands.

On television, Evan Fournier snagged a bounce pass from an Atlanta player and took it down court for an easy two.

Jim retrieved the gun, put it back in the bag, and placed it behind the sofa.

The day after David flew back to Sacramento, Jim noticed the bag was gone.

Truth be told, Angela feared Evan more than she had ever feared anything in her life. She had watched as his slow-burn temper rose to the boiling point after which he would seek malicious revenge. Three years earlier, when they were still married, Evan came home ranting about another Charlotte dentist. "That's the third client he's stolen from me this month," he yelled to no one in particular. "He can't just come into my 'hood and snag my customers."

"Maybe if you talked with him, Evan..."

"C'mon Angie. That would never work. Guys like this only know one thing. Brute force. We've gotta punch back and punch back hard. He's gotta feel it."

Evan floated a rumor — actually, had his hygienist, who would later steal Evan away from her, spread the word — that he was selling prescriptions. He also filed a concern with the North Carolina State Board of Dental Examiners. It didn't matter that there was no truth to the reports. They all but ruined the poor guy. Within six months he moved out of state. The last thing Evan heard was he was selling used cars in Texas.

If Angela threatened Evan, she knew he would do whatever he could to get revenge and she might never see Emma again. But she also knew she had to do something. She needed sound, informed advice about how to handle men who physically abuse their families. She needed to find someone she and Emma could talk with.

Sitting alone in the ER break room, she swiped her cell phone on with a shaking finger and prepared to contact Child Protective Services. Perhaps they could provide names of adolescent therapists. Before she could press the dial button, the phone in her hand rang, startling her, and she dropped it to the hard table surface. When she snatched the phone back, she saw a spider web of cracks across the top half of her screen, distorting the notification that Pam Reynolds was calling. She cursed under her breath. At least the phone still worked. She touched the "Answer" button.

"Hi, Angie," Pam said. "Are you busy?"

Angela calmed her shaking hands. "Well... no, not really. I'm on break."

"I just wanted to check in. I picked Emma and Taylor up at school and we're at the mall. Had a wonderful dinner at Cheesecake Factory and the girls are shopping right now."

"Thank you, Pam. I appreciate the update." Her palms felt damp as sponges and her chest was ready to explode.

"Guess what I'm doing right now," Pam said. "I'm having one of the most scrumptious slices of decadent cheesecake I've had in years."

"How does Emma seem tonight?"

"Fine. Happy. They're acting like silly little thirteen-year-olds. Why?"

Angela paused. She had to get it out. "I talked with Emma about those marks you mentioned... on her arm?"

"Oh, yes. Is she all right?"

"I'm afraid it's pretty serious."

"Oh, dear."

"She's having problems... with her father." And then it poured out. "Oh, Pam. He's so mean to her. He's hurt her... He hits her... She has bruises..."

"Oh, poor Emma. How can anybody be so cruel? You don't think he's done something, uh, you know, sexual?"

"No. At least, that's what she said. I have to try to believe her."

"Thank God."

A noise at the break room door broke her train of thought for a moment. "I just don't know what to do."

"Is there someone you can report this to?"

"Yes, I'm going to call Child Protective Services... They can help us get a counselor. They can tell me what I need to do to end visitations. We will have to insist on changes. We'll need an attorney. Things may get very ugly soon."

"Angie, how can I help?"

"You are helping already. Just being able to say it out loud is a help."

"Should I talk with Emma?"

"Oh, heavens, no. Don't say a word to Emma. And please keep it a secret from Taylor as well."

"Whatever you want. Let me know if there's anything..."

"Thank you, Pam. I really should be getting back."

"Okay. I'll take Emma and Taylor to school in the morning. Remember, you can always call me."

Angela's palms were sweaty and her shoulders were tight when she stood from the table and disconnected the phone. Her break was over and she needed to return to the ER, so she shoved the phone into her scrubs while reaching for the door handle.

"Oh, Dear!" the volunteer with well-coifed hair and way-too-much makeup said, from the other side of the doorway. "I was just taking my break..."

"Oh, yes. You are..."

"I'm Peggy Crutchfield. I usually volunteer in the main lobby... in reception. But, sometimes I like to take my break here... There's so much more going on. I find it so exciting."

How long had she been there? What had she heard? "Excuse me. I have to get back to work. After all, there is so much going on," Angela said, muscling her way through the doorway and scurrying down the hall.

CHAPTER NINE

Jim returned to the homeless shelter several times. He loved it. It was like manning a lighthouse on an island, rescuing drowning people, and he was the assistant keeper of the light. Those drowning came there for shelter, food, and safety. On each visit, he became more familiar with some of the regulars. Jim was feeling okay. They welcomed him. They accepted him. Maybe they even knew him.

Arriving during dinner, he stepped into the dining hall to greet the guests. Tonight they housed many of the regulars, like the young man who claimed to have over a hundred fathers as his eyes darted back and forth, and Red Fred the reader, who talked nonstop about the latest Jack Ryan novel. Jim greeted them each, chatting them up like long-time friends.

That's when Jim saw Skinny Santa. Sitting at a table on one side of the room, the old man with the long, scraggly beard stared directly at him. Patches of hair peeked through holes in a blue ski cap on his head, like tufts of crabgrass on a poorly manicured lawn. Jim approached the table, happy to see the old guy who, in a way, had sparked his interest in volunteering. He pulled up a chair across from him. "Hello, Gene."

The old man looked up, cocked his head, and studied Jim for a moment with a blank expression on his dirt-covered face. "Do I know you?"

Taken aback, Jim peered closer, thinking he may have mistaken this man for the one he shared coffee with several weeks earlier. "C'mon, Gene. I'm Jim Bishop. You and I had coffee in a coffee shop up town. Remember?" He wondered if the old man was playing a trick on him.

The man's eyes clouded over, as if from cataracts. "No. I don't think I know you." He returned to his meal, sopping up gravy with a biscuit.

Maybe Gene had a memory issue — some sort of dementia. But Jim was insistent. "Sure you do. It was a cold day. The place was packed. We talked over coffee."

Gene raised his eyes again and a faint glimmer crossed his eyes. "Yeah. I 'member... That coffee was all right."

Relieved he wasn't losing his mind, Jim sat back in his chair and said, "So how've you been?"

"Good."

"Have you seen your ex-wife lately... down in Filbert?"

Gene shook his head. "Nope. No reason to go there."

The conversation was strange, stilted, reminding Jim of his first year at UNC when he approached an upperclassman and tried to strike up a conversation. He had met the guy during rush and felt they had a lot in common. This time, however, he gave Jim a frown, turned to his frat brothers who were gathered around him and shrugged. "Anybody here know this guy?" Someone said something about a confused frosh punk and everyone laughed. Jim walked away feeling more than rejected... he felt shunned. He didn't like that feeling. He didn't pledge that guy's fraternity, either.

"Well," Jim said, getting up. "Let me know if you need anything."

"Why?" Gene asked, eyes on the food he shoveled into his mouth.

"Huh?"

"Why should I let you know?" He stirred the food around on his plate.

Jim leaned over, both hands resting on the chair back. "'Cause I'm here to help." If anyone, Gene should have known that already.

"And how can you help me?"

Jim, defensive, said, "Well, I can get you some clean socks, or a toothbrush, or some more desert..."

"That what you do around here?"

"Yeah," Jim answered. "Among other things. It helps me get to know the people staying here." He sat back down.

Gene ground his jaw from one side to the other. "Hmmm."

Jim felt challenged. He had treated this old geezer quite well that cold morning several weeks earlier, and now he was giving Jim grief. "The last couple of weeks, I've gotten to know lots of the people here," he said.

"Who?"

Jim searched the room, forced to prove himself — the zookeeper leading the tour group. "See that guy over there?" He pointed at a bald man with a massive belly a couple of tables over. "We go outside and shoot hoops when it's not too cold." Jim waved.

The big guy waved back, "Mr. B. How's it goin'?"

Jim smiled.

Gene frowned and Jim felt like he was being called out. He turned to his left and pointed to a couple of men down the way. "We played poker last time I was here. And I bought a new phone charger for that guy over there." He turned around in his chair and pointed toward the food line. "That guy who just picked up his plate... He's a drummer. Played with a rapper named Half-a-Dollar, I think."

"50 Cent."

"Whatever." It occurred to Jim that he didn't need to justify his behavior to Gene. He didn't need to prove himself to anybody. He wasn't an employee. He was there voluntarily, and volunteers didn't have performance reviews. He sat back, arms across his chest.

"Sounds like you're making the rounds," Gene said.

"Like I said, I've made some good friends here in the shelter. I'm just saying hello."

"So you wanna help these folks?"

"Yeah."

"You think they want your help?"

"Yeah. They all seem to appreciate it."

"How do you know that?"

"How does anyone know someone appreciates their help? They seem happy when they see me. They are friendly. You saw that. They say they appreciate it." It all seemed obvious.

"So, Mr. Jim. You like helping people when they appreciate it, right?"

Jim stopped cold. "Well, I like helping people all the time."

Gene slid his half-eaten dinner aside and leaned forward on his elbows. His eyes lit up. "The question is... are you here for them or are you here for you?" His eyebrows rose.

"What the hell are you talking about?"

"I was watching you earlier. Are you here 'cause they need your help or 'cause you need to be needed?"

"That's crazy!"

"Is it?"

Holding his hands up in resignation, Jim said, "So now you're gonna lecture me?" This was stupid — the helpless goading the helper.

Gene smiled and that's when Jim noticed one of his upper teeth was missing. "Just my humble opinion."

"I thought you appreciated my help."

"It ain't got nothin' to do with appreciation. If you really wanna help, you help. Don't expect nothin' in return."

Caught red-handed, Jim sat still. The old guy was right. Reaching out to those in need gave him a good feeling, but until now, he had been naive. He lived for the favor. And he'd failed to be like his wife, Jean. She gave to others because she could. Period.

"Jimbo. Don't help a man 'cause he will do something for you. Just help him." He stood up. "That's the end of the lecture," he said with a wink and then leaned forward. "Yes, this will be on the final." He chuckled as he walked toward the door, leaving his plate behind.

Jim stared at the dirty plate and silverware. The old man had left it there knowing someone would take it to the kitchen and wash it. He didn't care who would do that. The shelter wasn't a lighthouse on an island. It was a lifeboat, filled to overflowing with people who needed help. And Jim was right in there with them.

He picked up the plate and took it to the kitchen.

• • •

A gentle knock on his office door prompted Allen to look up to see Greg Johnston, the chairman of the staff relations committee in the doorway. The chairman and his committee were Allen's immediate bosses; they determined his and the other staff members' needs, benefits and compensation and offered guidance in their jobs.

Allen rose and welcomed the gray-templed man. They had a good relationship. Of course, there'd been a couple of tussles now and then, mostly over staffing requests, but they had solid rapport based on shared goals for the church.

After the usual kind words of greetings, the chairman thanked Allen for his time and said, "I talked to the District Superintendent today. He was thinking about moving the minister from Hickory over here to our church and moving you to Greensboro. Said their church might be a better fit for you." He seemed to watch Allen's face for a response.

"Really? He didn't call me." Since Superintendents usually spoke with ministers before going to the local church committee, Allen wondered if the chairman had reached out to the superintendent first. "I'm surprised. I thought the church was heading in the right direction."

The chairman looked about the office as if searching for the words. "Well, generally, I would agree, but you know this might be the best thing. Some of our church members have suggested we need someone with stronger pulpit skills."

The words were code to a minister — A better preacher, an entertainer, someone who made church fun.

"And, you'd like Greensboro."

"What else have you heard from the congregation, Greg?" Allen appreciated their honest, sometimes blunt, conversations, but detested the idea that people were talking behind his back. If they had something to say, they should say it to his face... But then again, as much as he hated it, that was often the reality of working in a church.

"Some people have said you spend too much time on external programs, like the school outreach and the homeless shelter, and not enough time on visitation... and sermon prep."

It was a lot for Allen to take. "Let me talk with the D.S. and we'll go from there, okay?" On the other hand, a move to another city would give Paul a chance for a new start. He hated the thought of moving him in the middle of high school, but it might be a blessing in disguise.

"Of course. And if you want to meet with the committee, we'll be glad to call a special session."

The chairman left the office in quiet — quiet that made for deep consideration in such times.

•   •   •

In the semi-darkness of her office, long after everyone had gone home, Kerry examined spreadsheet after spreadsheet displayed on three screens before her. Two years ago productivity had reached its highest point. In addition, they were scouting for new clients and thinking of ways to diversify.

But lately things had become stagnant. She blamed department heads. They weren't pushing for the growth her company required. They seemed unmotivated. How to motivate a dozen directors — incentivize or threaten? Kerry always leaned toward the latter. It kept her closer to the results. And they needed good results. If they didn't show a consistent growth trend, they might not be as inviting an acquisition target...

Her cell phone vibrated. Few people had access to this number, one or two of the men in her life — she had no time for them right now — and the Board Chairman, Thomas Donnelly. She pressed the talk button. "Hello, Thomas. It's so nice to hear from you."

"Likewise, Kerry. I wanted to talk with you about next month's board meeting."

"Yes?"

"You may have heard, some of Bell's board members are concerned about the company's direction."

"No, Thomas. I hadn't heard, but I feel confident..."

"We're thinking you might be able to use some extra help."

Kerry took it in.

"We want some time on the agenda next month to talk about keeping you exclusively at the CEO position and bringing in a company president under you."

She searched for the words to express herself, but all she could think was she was being replaced — put out to pasture. "That sounds... intriguing, Thomas. Do you have anyone in mind?"

"Wagerin and Fitzgerald know of a man out west — Gary Brindle. He's CFO of First In Class Marketing."

Brindle was a first-class jerk.

"He's a real go-getter. We think his skills would balance with yours quite well."

"Interesting. I didn't know Brindle was looking."

"Everybody's looking for the right opportunity."

Kerry knew there was nothing else to say about the recommendation. "Okay. We'll be sure to make time at the board meeting to talk about this further."

"Sounds great, Kerry. You know, I think this could be just the thing we need to reach our potential."

For once, potential sounded like a death sentence.

"Nice talking with you, Kerry. I'll touch base again next week. Good bye."

CHAPTER TEN

Independence Park became one of Jim's regular hangouts. The hiking trails, peaceful pond, and the beautiful view of the Charlotte skyline beckoned him every day. The memorial to Lillian Arhelger, a scout leader who had given her life to save a Girl Scout at Glen Burney Falls in Blowing Rock, was a peaceful spot to think about Jean, the beauty of her life, the sad reality of her death, and the wonderful gifts they shared over the years.

And Peggy was there. The more they were together, the more he longed to be alone. Something about her — an aggressiveness or a nosiness — set him off. Once he managed to sneak away from the park before she saw him.

He wasn't so lucky this time. They sat together on a bench across from the reflecting pool as Michael and his dog played fetch.

"You know, I have enjoyed getting to see you these last few days," Peggy said.

"It's been nice."

"I was thinking... Michael and I would love to have you over for dinner sometime. He stays over on some nights when his mother and father want some 'alone time'," she said with air quotes and a wink.

Jim had to keep himself from rolling his eyes.

"I love cooking, but since I lost my husband, it doesn't make sense for me to make a big meal when I'm by myself. But when Michael comes over we enjoy good, healthy food... and it would be nice to share it with you."

"As nice as that sounds, I think my volunteer work at the shelter might get in the way." He was feeling crowded and closed in, which surprised him. Maybe he just wasn't ready...

She placed her hand on his arm. "It's just that Michael would love having you over some evening. You're simply so good with him."

"No, Peggy. He's simply so good." He sought to change the subject and asked, "Have you seen much of Angela Griffen lately?"

She removed her hand from his sleeve. "Oh, she's sooo busy... She's got a lot on her plate."

"I'll bet she does. She's very good at her job."

"She also has a lot more going on behind the scenes," Peggy said. "I heard she's having trouble with her daughter."

"Oh?" Jim sensed where the conversation was going and he didn't like it. Out of politeness, he held his tongue.

"Don't tell anyone, but I heard that her ex-husband is a real scumbag."

"Well, I imagine..."

"I heard he treats their daughter very badly. Someone told me he may have molested her." Her eyes opened wide.

Jim froze. He eased his hands from his lap to the bench beneath him and squeezed the wooden slats. "What?"

"You didn't hear it from me," she went on, "but I understand she's talking with the authorities."

His knee was bouncing as if on a spring. Anyone who harms a young teenager should receive the worst punishment.

"But that could just be the rumor mill at the hospital. You know how those things go."

"Uh, yeah."

"If you're really interested, I could ask around. Maybe we could talk about it when you come over for dinner..."

He left her remark alone. They sat in silence.

She stood to go. "I really must get back to fix dinner for Michael," she flashed a wink and a smile.

Jim gave a half-wave goodbye and stared at the reflecting pool. After a bit, he looked down and noticed a splinter buried in his finger, a pool of blood surrounding the thin shard. He pulled his hand up and bit the tip of his finger, pulling the fragment out. He sucked away the blood and then pushed the finger against his thumb. He didn't separate the two until long after the bleeding stopped.

. . .

In his apartment, Todd sat alone. He had opened the sliding glass doors. The cold air somehow reassured him.

He couldn't recall how long he had been there, staring out the window into the evening blackness... not moving... not being able to move. In the dark, anything lit stood out like a beacon. Windows, streetlights, stop lights all glowed in the misty night air. But the lights were far away, and the apartment was shadowy and empty. One by one, the lights outside his windows disappeared. It was like the cave of evil on Dagobah, in Star Wars. It was black and dangerous. That guy in the gray hood was probably out there. Watching...

Todd picked up the lighter that lay on the end table beside him. Flashing it on, he held it under the meaty flesh of his left hand until the skin turned bright pink. Then he picked up the sewing needle sitting in a nearby ashtray and picked at the seared flesh. The pain would have been excruciating to most people.

He continued to stare out the window.

CHAPTER ELEVEN

He knew getting the gun would not be easy.

Todd walked into the local sporting goods store, checking out tents, fishing equipment, and an assortment of strange-looking survival gear in his quest. Since he wasn't athletic and had no interest in sports, such stores were foreign to him. He could count on one hand the number of times he'd been inside one. Maybe if he'd spent more time with his father, playing baseball or going to watch the Panthers, he would have learned his way around these stores. Maybe they would have gone hunting with Dad's friends and he would have learned to shoot. Instead, he stayed in his basement playing computer games. So, he had a hard time finding the firearms section. In the past, he had given little thought to gun rights issues, letting the government determine if someone should or should not have one, which type, and how they might use it. Such things weren't a part of his universe, resulting in a lack of understanding about how one might buy one... or how one might use one. His stalker probably had a gun — maybe several. Head down, he surveyed the black and silver pistols through the gleaming glass of the cabinet.

"Can I help you?" asked a clerk in a dark blue golf shirt with the store logo on his chest.

"Oh, uh, I was thinking about buying... you know, one of these." He looked down in the case feeling his face warm, feeling like the proverbial fish out of water.

"We've got the best handguns in the state."

"Uh, huh," Todd murmured. He scanned the hardware before him, not sure of what he needed.

"Why a handgun? What do you want to do with it?" the man behind the counter asked.

Todd lifted his palms from the glass surface, leaving a damp palm impression behind. He always sweated when he was nervous. "Security, mainly," he said, which sounded legit.

"Do you shoot much?"

"Enough," he lied.

The clerk nodded and slid a business card across the case. "If you need a little practice, try these guys. They have good handgun classes."

Todd stared at the card. A drawing of a red and black target sat dead-center below the name of a nearby shooting range. He pictured himself standing behind a half-height wall, aiming at the little circles on the piece of paper fifty yards away, and missing every shot. Much more experienced shooters around him would laugh and he'd be reminded again that he was a loser. However, this was important.

The employee walked Todd through the various makes and versions of the guns in the case, taking several out one at a time so Todd could handle them. He had no idea if one was better than another and was surprised at how heavy each was. He wondered why someone hadn't invented a video game in which the controls for shooting were heavier, more realistic. He could probably write the code for that. Of course, somebody else had probably already thought of that and he really wasn't that great a programmer after all.

The black Walther PK380 looked reliable to Todd — not too big or complex. "I'll take that one," he said without checking the price sticker. "And some bullets."

"Good. She's a beaut. Let me see your driver's license. You have your gun permit with you, right?"

Todd was reaching to his back pocket to retrieve his wallet, but stopped midway. "Gun permit?"

"Yep. In North Carolina you gotta have a completed gun permit, approved at the Sheriff's Office, to buy a handgun."

Todd took a step back, like the guy had just threatened to shoot him with one of the revolvers in the case. "I didn't know that." He should have checked it out online. How could he have been so stupid? They'd never approve a gun permit since the manslaughter ruling.

"Yeah. It's a pain, but that's the first step. It's pretty easy. Takes about a week or two to process."

Todd turned to go, mind whirling. Two weeks was about two weeks too long. He couldn't wait.

"But if you're dead-set on getting a gun..."

Todd eased back around.

"You don't need a permit to purchase a long gun."

"Long gun?"

"Yeah, a rifle." He reached behind him and pulled a Henry Rep Arms H001T from the rack. "This is one of my favorites. Easy to maintain. Uses 22 caliber bullets, which are great for target practice or rabbit hunting, and it's a real good rifle for someone just starting out. I gave one to my son just last Christmas." He handed it across the glass case to Todd. "And it's ideal for protection. One look at this and the bad guys run in the other direction."

Todd accepted the weapon from the salesman hesitantly and balanced it in his hands. He pulled the stock to his shoulder like the guys in the movies did and aimed down the sight at the floor, which he thought someone who was buying a rifle would do. The barrel seemed long, but not longer than any of the other rifles on the rack. Maybe he'd be able to pull this off after all.

"Or, if you'd prefer, you can try a shotgun," Blue Shirt said.

That would be too messy. "No, this will do just fine."

"Okay. I'll need your driver's license again. Fill out this paperwork. We can register this fine piece of hardware in your name right now."

Once again he had no idea of the process. Would registration alert authorities about his purchase and bring them pounding on his door before he even got home, for fear he just might shoot... someone? "Well, you know, I think I'll hold off on this," aware that it made him appear suspicious. He handed the rifle back to the surprised employee. "Yeah. I've gotta be somewhere... at a meeting in a few minutes." That sounded even more suspicious. He didn't care. He only wanted to get out of there as fast as possible.

"Okay. Ask for me when you come back."

It was all Todd could do to keep from charging out the door. All the security cameras in the store stood out like gun turrets, threatening to stop him in his tracks. When he reached his car, he sat in the driver's seat shaking, blaming himself for yet another major screw-up, convinced no one would sell him a gun in that store, or any store.

Berating himself on the drive home, he almost missed the pawn shop. A placard out front announced, "We Got You're Gun Right Here." He ignored the grammatical errors and pulled into the parking lot, dodging the cracked asphalt and potholes that threatened to ruin his tires.

He opened the door and immediately felt as out of place as if he was ten years old and had just walked into a porn shop. The inside was dark and smelled dusty. The concrete floor reminded him of a jail cell. A couple of other customers were browsing through some items in the back. One was small, wearing a wife beater undershirt beneath a leather jacket. His hair was cropped short, like tough guys in the movies. He raised his head when Todd opened the door, but Todd looked away to avoid making eye contact. The other guy was lanky, about six feet tall. He wore a baseball cap turned backwards, covering his shaved head, and a Tom Petty sweatshirt. He seemed oblivious to everything around him, including Todd. The store was full of old televisions, stereos, lamps, tables. A big black safe was behind the counter, dust covering its upper surface. Two glass cases displayed glimmering jewelry. A third held pistols.

Todd approached the counter hesitantly, not wanting to repeat his earlier failure and mumbled, "Uh, I'd like to see some of your guns."

The guy behind the counter lowered the hunting magazine he was reading, didn't say anything, but looked irritated, as if Todd was disrupting him. "Which one?"

He found a small Colt Mustang and weighed it in his hands. It seemed lighter than the ones he had checked out in the sporting goods store. Holding it up with both hands, he eyed down the sight toward the lock on the safe, convinced this one would do the trick, unless... He saw the piece of paper taped to the inside of the case. "Gun permits required for all handguns."

Setting the pistol on the glass top with a thunk, he turned for the door, shoulders slumped and head down, feeling like the loser he was.

"Well, do you want it or not?" the pawn shop salesman called. Todd ignored him, feeling rejected, like he had when he'd asked for a new computer for Christmas and his father said he was too young. "You don't need a computer, son. Go outside and play baseball."

He had just opened his car door when he heard a call from behind him. "Hey! Hang on there, man."

Todd turned to see the short guy in the leather jacket coming toward him. "I noticed you're lookin' for a gun," he said in a lower voice.

Todd closed the car door.

"The damn Feds don't make it easy to exercise our Second Amendment Rights these days. I know that. My cousin tried to buy a gun, but just because he and his wife argue a little, he couldn't get a permit. I found him a Glock and the government couldn't do anything to stop me. And I can get you a gun, too." He lowered his head a little, as if watching for Todd's reaction.

Todd's heart pounded in his chest. He'd never done anything like this before. He searched the parking lot for security cameras, wondering if the transaction might be recorded or if some security force might swoop down from the sky to arrest him for purchasing a firearm without a permit. "I'm listening."

"I just happen to have a sweet little Remington R51," he said, emphasizing R. Five. One, "in my truck right there." He pointed toward a battered Ford pickup. "I'll let ya have it for a thousand."

Todd scoffed. "They cost just three fifty in there." He nodded toward the pawnshop.

"Yeah, but mine don't require a note from your mama."

Todd's upper lip felt cold from sweat. "Let's see it." He scanned the parking lot for police.

In the shade of the pickup, the guy displayed the handgun like a jeweler showing a diamond. But it wasn't a diamond. The scratches and brushed marks on the handle suggested it might have been tossed out of his truck window once or twice and run over once or twice. Somebody had scratched off the serial number.

"This baby will stop any bad guy who messes with you." One eyebrow rose.

Todd had no way of knowing if the guy was taking advantage of him. "How do I know it works?"

"There ain't much that can stop a gun from working. It's just a firing pin and a barrel, but if you want to test it, we can go over to the quarry and take a shot or two."

Todd wondered if the quarry was safe or if the guy might jump him and leave his body in some murky lake never to be found, which was probably what he deserved. In the end, he went to the bank, withdrew a thousand dollars, and met the guy at the quarry where they fired the Remington several times. The guy showed Todd how to hold the gun correctly in a patient and careful way, like he'd done this many times before. Obviously, he respected the fire power of the pistol. He accepted Todd's wad of hundreds and said, "If you want a shotgun... I know a guy..." Todd turned him down, turned around, and drove off with the R-Five-One and a half a box of bullets sitting on the passenger seat. His heart pounding in his chest, he half expected a SWAT team to be waiting outside the quarry to take him to jail.

Sitting in the darkness of his apartment with the sliding glass door open, he thought about the short man and the gun. He had just paid a thousand dollars for an old, beat up pistol. The guy was probably laughing at him, telling his buddies over a round of beers about the stupid guy who bought his old, beat up pistol. People had always laughed at him, like the time in high school when he blurted out, "I love you," to the head cheerleader in front of the whole cheering squad. Like when he had lost his job at Bell. Like when he'd killed the cyclist. They always laughed. And why not? After all, he was a screw-up.

Wondering if the stalker was outside his apartment watching, he squinted his eyes and picked out the dark figure across the street. *Could be the same guy* — skinny, hood covering his head. He seemed small. Todd wondered how long he had been standing there. "Get ready for the surprise of your life, Dude." He aimed the R-Five-One out the open doorway.

This just might be the best thing I'll ever do.

He waited in the dark apartment alone. A plane roared by overhead.

Then he pulled the loaded R-Five-One to his temple and pulled the trigger.

. . .

For several nights in a row, Sheryl had watched his apartment. This was *important* — worth standing in the cold night air. She wanted to tell the man about the accident, that he didn't do nuthin', that someone had blamed him just like her husband had blamed her when they ran out of cash and were thrown out of their home. She wished somebody had told her she didn't do nuthin' back then. It would have changed things — it would have made a difference.

Old Fred Jackson, he went by Red — Red Fred, that's funny — told her about the innocent man. Red Fred always read newspapers. He usually got them in the library, or the coffee shops, or by begging them off strangers, but he read... a lot. Then he shared the news with others under the bridge near the shelter. He had read how this man was accused of running over that man on a bike.

She heard the story and knew it was wrong. The man — Todd somebody or other — hadn't run over that guy. She'd seen it with her own eyes. A lady in a fancy black car had done it. The man came along after that woman. His car didn't even touch the biker.

She tried to ignore the story for a long time, but couldn't get it out of her head. It took weeks to find Todd Sanders. She searched for him like she had searched for Danielle — walking the streets, searching in car windows, checking out fancy-dressed people walking into the fancy buildings uptown. Finally, Red looked him up on the computer in the library for her, leading her here. Now she just had to figure how to get to him and tell him the God awful truth. He hadn't done nuthin'.

It was cold, again, like the night before. She pulled the little string on the hood tight so it covered more of her face and hugged the baby in her belly and stomped her feet to chase away the chill. Maybe she'd walk up the steps and knock on that door. She'd tell him and run away. Run back to the shelter. She could do that. Just say it and run away.

She watched the dark apartment. A plane rumbled overhead.

The gunshot blast reverberated over the sound of the plane. The bright flash of light shattered the darkness.

She was too late.

CHAPTER TWELVE

A voice came over the ER loudspeaker. "Attention. We have a Code Black-J. Repeat. Code Black-J. All available staff come to the ambulance bay. Repeat. Code Black-J in the ambulance bay."

Angela flung the door open.

The ambulance squealed to a stop mere inches from the emergency room door and a stretcher, wheels bumping along the tile floor, rushed through the entrance toward the trauma rooms. Hospital attendants ran through the lobby. Frantic voices shouted inaudible phrases over each other as the rolling gurney slid behind swinging doors. Angela joined the rush, helping the crew care for the young man, trying not to stare at the side of his head which had been ripped open. Blood, liquid, and chunks of brain mixed with bone clung to his bleached hair. She did notice the burns on the fleshy bottom of his hand and thoughts of Emma threatened to cloud her mind, but she pushed them back... for awhile.

It wasn't good — obviously a gunshot to the temple. Chunks of white cranial bone were embedded into a mass of gray brain matter. Even though Angela had seen wounds like this before, the sight made her cringe. A vein opened up, spitting blood on the doctor's shirt. It was clamped shut. The man's heartbeat slowed and then stopped. Someone shouted orders and electric paddles were slapped to his chest and his body lurched from the shock. Again. The heartbeat came back, faint. More people shouted. The heartbeat stopped again but further resuscitation efforts were unsuccessful. They kept trying. Again. Again.

The frenetic activity in the trauma room came to a halt and everyone exhaled in one breath. The doctor pronounced the young man dead and stated the time. One by one people backed away from the body, removed gloves and masks, and shuffled toward the door.

Angela felt a familiar ache in her neck as she entered the hallway. She rotated her head to stretch out the kink, first left then right, but it didn't help much. She was heading to the locker room to clean up and refresh her scrubs when she happened a glance through the small window in the door that led to the emergency room. Outside a lone figure waited. It couldn't be a friend or family member — they would have come inside to hear the news — the bad news. The person just watched the front door.

Angela turned and pushed through the double doors with a thump. A guard was standing near the exit, staring at the lone observer.

She had to talk with the watcher.

. . .

She watched. Sheryl knew the Wesley Memorial Hospital Emergency Room well. She had been there twice before — once for pneumonia and another time after some rich kids had beat her up. She didn't like the Emergency Room.

Now, Mr. Todd was in there. He was hurt.

She stood outside in the chilly night, dancing from one foot to the other. Left. Left. Right. Right. The Dance of the Lost. A guard stared out the glass doors so she turned her back afraid that he might chase her and find the gun.

Sheryl had run inside Todd's apartment through the glass doors, screaming after he shot himself.

He was lying on the floor on his side. Blood was everywhere. He was hurt. He was hurt bad.

The gun lay on the floor near him. Sheryl reached for it... Picked it up, afraid somebody else might find it and somebody else might get hurt.

A voice in the hallway shouted, "Somebody call 911." Pounding on the door.

Police would come. They would take her baby.

Sheryl stuffed the gun into one of the sweatshirt pockets... to keep it from hurting anyone else.

She turned and ran back through the open patio door, knowing they would take him to Wesley Memorial Hospital. She ran down the street toward the hospital. She had to tell them Todd hadn't killed the man on the bicycle.

An ambulance passed her before she reached Wesley.

She had stood outside the emergency room doors for a long time. A guard blocked the entrance so she couldn't go inside. Her hands were cold. She hugged her belly to keep the baby warm.

When she looked again, the guard was gone.

He was replaced by an angel dressed in green, but she didn't stand behind the glass door. She came out into the cold. "Hello? Hello?"

Sheryl turned to go.

"Wait," the nurse lady said. "Do you know anything about the man who was just brought in? Were you the one who reported it?"

Sheryl waited. "He ain't done nuthin'."

"What?" The nurse lady came closer.

"He didn't do it." She pulled her gray sweatshirt around herself, protecting her baby and hiding the gun.

"Do what? Shoot himself? Is that what you're saying?"

Sheryl shook her head — hard.

"What didn't he do?" the nurse lady asked again. She was closer.

"I gotta go."

"Wait. You may be able to help."

Sheryl turned and ran away. She had protected her baby. She had hidden the gun in her sweatshirt pocket. She might need it to protect her baby.

CHAPTER THIRTEEN

When he was a kid, Jim thought funeral homes were spooky places where mysterious people did mysterious things to other mysterious people. That may have been one reason why he avoided funerals in his younger years. The halls were dark and dusty, the music creepy, and everyone seemed so morbid.

Now, he realized that the facility itself brought home the reality of death — revealing in a gentle, humane way, that a life was no more, that a soul had passed, and that it was time to grieve. The ornate candelabras above gave off subdued light, and the soft, padded chairs, the pseudo-stained glass windows, and the almost imperceptible music lulled Jim into a trance-like state. At Todd's funeral, there was no casket, only a decorated urn on a stately table before the rows of chairs, muting the horrible, grisly nature of his death — suicide by gunshot and the damage a firearm discharge had made.

When he felt the presence of someone else on the row next to him he looked up into the kind and welcome eyes of Rev. Allen Rhodes who took the seat beside Jim and whispered, "How'd you know Todd?"

"We met at the shelter. You?"

"I met him after he'd had an accident with a bicyclist a few months back. Saw him at the shelter, too. Seemed like such a good guy."

"He told me about that. It really tore him up. I can't imagine going through something like that."

Allen nodded. "That sort of thing will change you, and only in a bad way."

Searching the ornate chapel, Jim glanced toward the doorway just as Angela Griffen appeared. He smiled and waved her over. In quiet whispers he introduced her to Allen and she mentioned she had been in the ER when Todd was admitted after his suicide attempt. She was with him when he died.

Very few others were at the service. A handful of young adults, perhaps members of Todd's church, sat together toward the front. A young man about the same age sat on the row opposite them with an older man whom Jim assumed was his father.

As the minister of *Living Waters* approached the podium and the ushers moved to close the doors, a lone figure, dressed in black with a dark veil, slipped into the back corner seat. Jim leaned back and watched her over his shoulder. Kerry Noland's sniffles could be heard throughout the chapel as she dabbed her eyes beneath the veil, wiping away tears and mascara. She was always drawn to drama, so Todd's death may have been just another melodramatic fix for her... a pathetic one.

After a brief greeting, two young adults took the stage and sang a modern version of an old hymn in perfect two-part harmony, gesturing with subtle hand motions accompanied by looks of compassion and sincerity. The music rose in intensity and sobbing from the back of the chapel became louder. Jim glanced over his shoulder and saw Kerry, head down, shoulders shaking as she wept. He felt compelled to help, despite the way she had treated him in the past. It could have been an opportunity for him to help, without expecting anything in return, which Gene had challenged him to do. But an usher, dressed in muted grey suit and matching tie, arrived before Jim could move and placed a box of tissues on the empty seat beside her. Her cries became louder.

The minister's message was generic and uninspiring, and the service ended. Jim, Angela, Allen, and the small crowd exited the building, Kerry dashed for a limousine waiting by the curb — refuge from the reality in the chapel.

Standing in the shadow of a large oak on the other side of the parking lot, a frail woman, dressed in a gray, hooded sweatshirt and ragged jeans, stepped forward as the small funeral crowd looked on.

"I seen you!" she shouted. "You were there. You did it! I know you did it. You in the fancy car. You are guilty."

Kerry froze, staring over the top of the limousine at the woman who marched toward her and continued to shout, "You are a bad woman. You are evil. You killed that man on the bicycle." The hooded woman kept walking toward her, accusing finger at the end of the woman's short arm, targeting her like Death, himself.

Out of the corner of his eye, Jim saw a young adult, one he recognized from the service, step to the sidewalk. He was slender and tall, with spiky blond hair. At first Jim thought he might try to stop the homeless woman, but the man's trajectory was toward the limo. Someone from the crowd behind him yelled, "Steve! What are you doing?"

Jim headed for Kerry's limousine too, but before he could reach the vehicle, the doors slammed shut and it sped away. The young man stood transfixed, stiff arms ending in clenched fists and shoulders bent forward like a boxer leaning into a powerful punch. Across the parking lot, the woman in gray also stood still, staring after the limousine. A gust of wind parted the oak's limbs above her and bright sunlight revealed the utter disdain she had for the woman who rode away in the limo.

"That was intense," Angela said.

"Who was that?" Allen asked over Jim's shoulder.

"Kerry Noland. CEO of Bell Intelliservices. That's where Todd worked. I used to work at Bell, too. I think the guy over there by the curb works there now. And the woman across the lot... I met her at a homeless shelter. I don't know if Todd knew her from there or not."

Angela said, "I saw her at the hospital the night they brought him in... after the suicide," Her head drooped. "I had no idea who she was and I couldn't get her to come inside."

They turned from the spectacle that had just played out as two men, one about Todd's age and the other much older, walked through the door. Allen turned on his minister persona and introduced himself to the two. "I'm Jeremy Lichtner," Jim heard the young man say. "This is my dad, Dr. Lichtner. Todd was my best friend when we were kids."

"I'm so sorry. I know this must be devastating," Allen said. He introduced Angela and Jim to the couple. In the brief interaction, they learned Jeremy was now a teacher in Monroe, just south of Charlotte, and his father was a therapist on the east side of the city. "I grew up next door to Todd," Jeremy said. He gazed toward the sky as if trying to find his lost friend. "We played video games all the time. After college, I tried to stay in touch but we just sort of drifted apart." He lowered his eyes and said,

"I knew he was dealing with some tough stuff, but I didn't think it was this bad."

Allen looked him in the eye. "You can't really tell. Sometimes people hide their feelings..."

"I know."

"It was nice to meet you," Dr. Lichtner said. "I just wish it had been under different circumstances. Jeremy and I should be getting home." As they walked away, Angela hesitated and then followed them to their car where they talked some more. Jim saw Dr. Lichtner hand her a business card before driving away.

Jim turned to focus on Allen who had been staring into the trees beyond the parking lot for a while as if searching for someone. He said, "We may be moving to Greensboro soon."

"Really? Why?"

"The District Superintendent feels our church is ready for some new blood. It happens from time to time."

Jim said, "I hope it's a good move for you, but I, for one, am sure gonna miss your preaching." Both men chuckled.

"We'll just have to see how it goes. I guess my biggest concern is my son. You know, transitions like this, when you're a high school junior, can be really tough."

"I hear you. I wish there was some way I could help. Call me if I can do anything."

Allen nodded. "You know, I should be getting back to the church. I'll let you know about the Greensboro thing. If it happens..." A quick goodbye and Allen was in his car, pulling out of the parking lot.

It seemed to Jim that a season of change was in the air.

As Allen drove away, Angela approached from her brief visit with Dr. Lichtner.

"He seems like a nice man," Jim offered.

"Yes, he does. It's hard to imagine that something good may come out of a horrible tragedy like Todd's death, but sometimes it does." She tucked the business card in her purse and continued to stare toward the curb, deep in thought.

Jim forced himself to remain quiet for what seemed to be a long time, thinking Angela might want to talk. The silence was stifling.

"It's just my family... my daughter." She shrugged. "Emma's thirteen and facing the same stuff that all teenagers face... plus so much more. Todd Sanders' suicide is so frightening..."

Jim wrapped an arm around her shoulder. "Raising kids must be tough these days."

She leaned her head against his chest and said, "I'm so worried about her."

Jim took a deep breath. *Is this what Peggy was talking about?*

She backed up a half-step, placed her hand on his lapel, like Jean used to and said, "Her father, Evan, has her two nights a week. He coaches her softball travel team, so we coordinate their time around the team schedule."

Jim felt his shoulders tighten. Angela needed to talk, but he didn't want to hear about Evan's atrocious behavior.

"Evan is a mean man. He gets so angry. She said he's very mean to her when she makes a mistake in a game. He's purposefully hit her with a softball at batting practice more than once. He slaps her. He demeans her in front of her friends. I've seen the bruises."

Jim struggled to respond.

Angela sighed and closed her eyes, as if blotting out her thoughts. "I'm sorry. It's just the day, the funeral, Todd's sui... We'll be all right... eventually."

"If I can help...," Jim offered.

As they parted for their cars and separate lives, Jim reflected on the events of the day — the tragedy and the way it affected so many people, the way people's lives intersected, bringing judgement and pain, and the silent needs everyone carried with them.

Cars. Lined up like garbage cans on the curb on trash day. Doors opened and closed as people, dressed in dark colors, entered the funeral home. They didn't stay inside very long. She'd waited longer in a soup line on a cold, windy day.

Sheryl had known some of the people. The big man who talked with her at the shelter. He was nice. The nurse lady who was at the hospital. The man who stopped by the wreck to talk to the dead man — Todd. The lady — the driver... She had no idea who the others were, and she didn't care.

She hadn't known whether to run after them, to tell them Todd hadn't done nothin' wrong, or to stay quiet. Ultimately, she felt compelled to tell the truth, so she had hollered at the lady, but then the lady drove off.

She looked back to the group walking away. She felt sorry for Todd. He never knew he hadn't done it. Now, he'd never know.

A few people waited behind after the others left. The big guy from the homeless shelter, the man who stopped, and the nurse stood in front of the funeral home. Then one of the men left and the other two talked for a long time. They hugged before leaving in separate cars.

After everyone had driven away in their shiny garbage cans, Sheryl walked out of the darkness of the woods to the door of the funeral home. They weren't locked, and no one was inside, so she slipped through the big glass entrance. The urn containing Todd's ashes stood on the table in the front of the chapel. She stepped up to it and examined the surface — shiny, smooth, and curved. Pretty. Like a porcelain vase in a flower shop. She reached out her hand, dirty, skinny fingers poking through torn gloves, and raised the top of the jar to chance a peer inside, but it was too dark to see anything. "Mr. Todd? You in there? You need to know, you didn't do it. You didn't kill that man. You didn't do nothing." She wondered if he might talk back, but he didn't.

The sun was setting, so she took one last look at the vase before leaving for the tall buildings and the empty streets downtown.

CHAPTER FOURTEEN

After the funeral, Kerry left as quickly as she could. In her apartment, she changed into jeans and an old, faded red pullover and whipped out a quick email to the chairman of the board saying she felt it was necessary to take a temporary leave of absence due to personal and health issues. She threw a small bag of casual clothes into the back seat of her red Lexus. She turned off her cell. She left the radio off as well, and drove south. Alone.

Like almost every other interstate highway, I-74 barreled forward, flanked by nondescript forests, farmland and the occasional strip mall, gas station of fast-food restaurant, toward North Carolina's Brunswick Islands before veering east to Wilmington, where Hurricane Florence had come ashore a few years before. At Laurinburg, Kerry exited onto Highway 501, a bare shred of two-lane asphalt over sandy flatland. The road was empty, with only a solitary farmhouse or billboard every mile or so. Just past Rowland, 501 became Highway 130 and she knew she was getting closer. Up ahead, almost hidden from the rest of the world, was her childhood home of Fair Hope, North Carolina.

The name was fitting. Rumor was the town had been named in the days gambling was legal in North Carolina, back in the 1700s. A gambler took a chance, and hoped his best was better than the rest. A good risk could lead to a win. That's what Alexander McRae did when he built a mill down on the Lumber River and the town rewarded him by being called Alexander. That's what Gus Smith did when he built the first hotel in the town to encourage tourists to visit. And that's what Kerry did so many years ago when she had nothing, took a risk, hoping to fool people into believing in her, and wound up as the CEO of a successful corporation.

That's also what she did on that rainy night in Charlotte. She took a risk that she wouldn't get caught and someone else would take the rap. Unfortunately, it was all catching up to her and she would be forced to ante up. Eventually the word would get out that she had killed the bicyclist on MLK and she would go to jail and lose everything she had invested in Bell Intelliservices. She'd be worthless. Like her failure of a father.

In a way this journey was like her father calling her home.

If someone took any southern downtown in any southern state and plopped it into the middle of Fair Hope, no one would notice. It would look the same. That is, before Hurricane Matthew devastated the area just six years earlier, making the city of one thousand a boarded up ghost town. Shuttered, first against the storms, and later against looters, stores along Main Street contained nothing — no products, no customers, no life. Two years later, Hurricane Florence piled on another load of devastation and destruction.

Kerry was home.

One of the few things she had taken from her elementary school education in Fair Hope was a line from one of Robert Frost's poems: "Home is the place where, when you go there, they have to take you in." But she wasn't even worthy to be taken in at Fair Hope and she wasn't looking for that. She simply needed a place to go. She didn't go to any of her usual getaway places: Vegas, or New York, or Barbados. Instead, she went home... where they had to take her in.

In the mid afternoon sunlight, she found her childhood house, a small shell of a structure, standing along a side street on the edge of town. Studs, burned black and jagged — the remnants left after a fire, jutted from the foundation like spires from an abandoned cathedral, reaching for the sky. The rest of the house looked to have been washed away by the storms. Weeds and overgrown bushes defined a yard that had been left alone for years.

It reminded her of her father — burned down and washed away — a failure in all he did. It was as if he had been cursed — cursed to fail at everything. He must have passed the curse on to her. Since her scapegoat,

Todd Sanders, had taken his life, hers had crumbled into failure. Staring at the house she felt empty, hollow, worth even less.

Driving back into town, a sign on the other side of the railroad tracks caught her eye. She turned left at the next intersection and left again onto Railroad Street, coming to stop before what looked like a twenties-era home, with a wrap-around, white picket-lined porch and yellow siding. A sign out front indicated it was the Fair Hope branch of the Columbus County Library. Surprised to find it relatively intact, she parked and entered the building. Several rows of books filled most of the interior, and a section of computers lined a wall in back.

A young woman, volunteer badge affixed to her sweater, met Kerry in front of the librarian's desk and asked if she could help. Kerry explained her situation: she had grown up in Fair Hope and was hoping to find information about her father. The volunteer steered her to an aging microfilm machine, next to a large cabinet of rolls of microfilm, and helped her find newspaper references to Jack (JC) Noland.

It didn't take long to find an article indicating JC had joined the 101st Airborne Division in late sixty-nine and had been sent to fight in Vietnam. He had attained the rank of sergeant, which surprised Kerry, and had served only one tour of duty. "Figures." All of her life she had been told her father was lazy, worthless, and couldn't keep a job. The fact that he'd only served one tour of duty just confirmed her image of him. The article indicated he had participated in something called the Battle of Fire Base Support Ripcord, and had been hospitalized shortly afterward.

Another article listed JC Noland among several other Vietnam soldiers. His name was the only one next to a small symbol of an eagle above the word, "Airborne".

The last article was an obituary from 1980. Jack (JC) Noland had committed suicide in his home in Fair Hope with a handgun.

Kerry lurched back in the small wooden chair and covered her mouth with her hands to prevent a threatening scream. Todd Sanders. JC Noland. The same fate. Tears fell onto the base of the microfilm machine and she sobbed out loud before collapsing onto the table. The volunteer rushed to her side but she brushed her away with a sweep of her arm.

In 1980, she lived far away in Raleigh where her mother had taken her after leaving Jack Noland for good. A middle school student, her mother must have chosen not to tell her about her father's suicide. She grew up assuming he had died an alcoholic in some gutter in Fair Hope. Now, she knew the truth.

Kerry arose slowly and turned away from the microfilm machine and trudged through the exit door, leaving the Fair Hope library behind and carrying the loser curse of her father with her.

The man looked ill — pale skin covered with sweat, bloodshot eyes, and shallow breath. He stopped scanning the clothing tags for Jim's purchase and leaned against the counter for balance.

"Are you all right?" Jim asked. He extended a hand for support. The store was crowded, as was the entire shopping mall. Easter was coming and shoppers were busy preparing for the event. Jim had joined the throng to pick up a navy blue sport coat and take advantage of the current clothing sales when he noticed the man at the register.

The store employee stared into Jim's face long enough to blink a couple of times before crumpling to the floor. Jim dropped to his knees to try to help. He loosened the man's tie, felt his sweaty forehead, and that was all he could think to do. He didn't know CPR or even how to identify a heart attack. "Help! Someone call 911!" he shouted. A small mob of shoppers grouped around them and watched. No one volunteered to help. No one dialed 911. "C'mon. You," he said to a woman eyeing the screen of her phone while obviously texting. "Damn it, call for an ambulance."

She looked startled, then tapped a few more letters before pulling the phone to her ear and reporting the incident to the operator on the other end of the line.

"Are any of you doctors? Does anyone know CPR?" Jim called into the crowd. No one moved.

Jim leaned down and placed his ear near the man's mouth to tell if he was breathing but he couldn't detect anything. He couldn't feel a pulse on his neck, either. He tried to do what he'd seen actors do in the movies, placing both hands on the man's chest and pumping hard, over and over. Then he held the man's nose, placed his lips against the man's, and breathed into his mouth. He repeated the action. Pump, breathe, pump, breathe.

While giving resuscitation, he peered through the legs of people in the crowd and watched a lady, carrying a bundle of new clothes, dash through the large glass doors into the parking lot. An alarm wailed but nobody seemed to notice.

Help arrived. Two men wearing pressed, white shirts with the word, "Security" embroidered over their left breast, pushed through the crowd surrounding Jim and the employee. A third guard rushed through the glass doors in search of the thief who had set off the alarm.

Jim sat back against the register counter and watched as the crowd dispersed. Shoppers picked over sale items on a table while others scrutinized clothing on nearby racks. One lady, shirt in hand from a nearby stack, turned to face the register desk, and flashed a frustrated frown before turning away in search of an open register. Others walked by pushing shopping carts, faces turned in his direction.

The glass doors whooshed open and two EMTs rushed in with a collapsible gurney. Jim slid aside a little, shocked at his own exhaustion. It took a lot of effort to try to save someone's life while keeping alive yourself.

Jim recalled that Jean had collapsed on a Charlotte sidewalk about six months earlier, but someone... homeless people he had never met... had stopped to help. No questions asked. They just tried to help.

The EMTs lifted the man onto the stretcher and rolled him out the doors toward the waiting ambulance. The crowd disappeared. One of the store security guards leaned over and placed a hand on Jim's shoulder. "You did the best you could do." He spoke with a slight accent. His name badge identified him as Jean Luc.

Shaking his head, Jim said, "I didn't know what to do."

"You did what you could, and that made a real difference." The security guard reached down and helped Jim stand.

Exhausted, Jim left the blue sport coat, the sale, and the store for his car in the parking lot and home.

Emma needed help. A lot of it. Angela's nursing training had taught her the importance of professional help, so she called Dr. Lichtner — he too was named Jeremy, like his son — and he recommended a colleague with the kind of expertise that would help Emma. "I've known Dr. Barbara Marks-Thompson most of my professional life and she is very good. She has a way of developing a strong and natural rapport with children and adolescents." His voice was confident and reassuring. "She can also put you in touch with attorneys who specialize in child abuse law. They can advise you as to how to keep your daughter safe, perhaps through a restraining order or by insisting on chaperoned family visits." Angela shivered at the thought of both of those ideas — They would require confronting Evan and that would make him angry. She hated him. She hated him more when he was angry.

Angela pressed Jeremy further. "I was also wondering if you might be available to help me... if I could make an appointment to talk with you about this. I feel like I'm under so much pressure..."

There was a pause. "I would be glad to add you to my client list," Jeremy said, "but, this isn't my area." He recommended another therapist.

Disappointed because she had felt comfortable with him since meeting him at the funeral, she thanked him for his advice and prepared to hang up when he interrupted her. "Angela. I may not be the right person to work with you as a counselor... but I would like to get to know you better. Please excuse me if I'm being too forward, but would you like to have dinner with me?"

The request came as a pleasant surprise. "Sure. Unfortunately, I work the late shift at the hospital."

"I'm sure we could find time. When do you have time off? We could meet for lunch if that would be better." They set the date for the next Thursday night and the two said their goodbyes. Angela's head spun as she thought of dating again. It had been awhile. A couple of disastrous blind dates with men who talked nonstop about themselves and a lunch date with a doctor from Pediatrics whom she later found was married, were her only experiences since she separated from Evan. Evan — the scum.

Jeremy, however, seemed like the best guy she'd met in a long, long time. Maybe the best ever. She forced herself to take things easy, lest she be hurt. Still, she found herself humming again during work, and basked in that feeling.

The incident in the mall looped in Jim's head, non-stop. The more he replayed the tape, the more angry he became. The apathy of the onlookers during the tragedy repulsed him, and his anger flowed over into other recent events in his life.

For some reason, Angela's situation with her daughter bubbled up to the surface. He didn't know many of the details, but based on what Peggy had said, and on Angela's actions at the funeral, something terrible was happening to her daughter, and her ex-husband appeared to be the cause. He liked Angela, and for that reason alone, whatever Evan had done made him angry. But without knowing more, he had no idea how he could help, and that was the very definition of helplessness.

He decided he needed to talk about his frustrations, so he contacted Allen Rhodes. He called his home, but Grace said he was at a nearby YMCA coaching a middle school basketball game. Jim arrived during the last three minutes of the fourth quarter. Allen was on the floor, huddled with a group of kids dressed in purple jerseys, talking them through their strategy for the rest of the game. Glancing at the score clock, he noted Allen's team was up by three.

They had the ball and Allen shouted at them to wait for the best shot. A guard passed it to the top of the key and to the guard on the other side setting up the big man who came across the lane, grabbed the bounce pass and hooked it in the basket, raising their score by two more points. Jim sat down in the visiting team bleachers. It had been a couple of years since he'd been to a Hornets basketball game and a lifetime since he'd seen middle school boys play ball. The rough surface of the wooden seat beneath him, the repetitive pounding of the basketball, and the squeak of tennis shoes against the floor brought him back to middle school.

A small group of girls leapt and shouted as their team headed back down the court for defense. They screamed with the zeal of professional cheerleaders. When the ball was stolen by a short guard with fast hands, their cheers urged him down the court at the speed of light — a brilliant purple flash heading for an easy layup.

Off to one side of the cheering throng, a young girl stood alone, arms crossed over her chest and prevented from cheering by some unknown force. Perhaps she faced some family trauma that stripped her of confidence and self-esteem. Maybe some selfish, demented adult relative was the cause...

The final buzzer sounded, Allen's team gathered in a victory cluster for final game advice and instructions, and the kids, along with a handful of adults and older youth, cleared the gym.

Jim and Allen met at one end of the court and Allen shot a gorgeous arching three pointer. Jim rebounded the ball, weighted it in both hands, and put up a shot that missed the rim by a foot. "Been a long time," he muttered.

The ball bounced back to Allen who dropped another three point shot. Nothing but net. "What brings you down here?" he asked.

"Your wife said you were coaching today. Looks like a heck of a team."

"They're a great bunch of kids," he said, whipping the ball behind his back and laying it up left-handed. *Showboat.*

Jim took a deep breath and said, "I heard something the other day that really bothered me and I thought I needed to talk to somebody... So, you're somebody." He smiled at his effort to lighten the conversation with a joke. "It's about Angela — the nurse you met at the funeral."

"Sure. Seemed very nice."

"I'll just be blunt. I've heard rumors about the way her ex-husband is treating their thirteen-year-old daughter."

Allen took a jumper that ricocheted off the rim.

Jim tried his best to relay what Angela had told him after Todd's funeral.

Allen's body seemed to have tensed up like a bowstring pulling back an arrow, in the seconds since Jim mentioned Emma. His next shot rolled around the rim twice before falling off.

"A lady who volunteers at the hospital told me she'd heard some terrible stories. In fact, she wanted me to believe it was much worse... but then, she does seem a bit hysterical." Jim took a shot from inside the key that fell in. "I don't know any of the details and it's all second or third hand news, so it may be nothing. But it has upset Angela."

Allen hung his head low and said, "That is absolutely terrible. I don't know how a man can be so evil to do that. You know, my son was her age not very long ago." He breathed in deeply and seemed to fade off into his own world for a moment, oblivious to everything around him.

"Allen?" Jim said.

Allen blinked. "You know the Bible says it would be better for a man to have a huge rock tied around his neck and to be thrown into the sea than to cause harm to a child."

The two men stood beneath the basketball goal, one holding the ball against his hip, and the other holding his breath while awaiting guidance. Jim tried a joke. "Any idea where I can get a huge rock and some rope?"

Allen breathed in, holding his anger at bay. "She needs to take whatever precautions she can."

"Like what? You're not suggesting she arm herself?" Jim had never been in a situation where he feared for his life... his job or his marriage, but never his life.

"That's up to her. Change the locks on her doors. Get a dog... a big dog. Stuff like that." His left hand clenched into a tight ball.

"I'll tell her..."

"Damn that makes me so mad!" Allen fired the ball into the empty bleachers where it bounced around like a pinball before lodging itself in the well between the rows of seats.

For the first time since Jim had met Allen, he felt scared of his friend. He had no idea a minister could get so angry. Then, Allen seemed to transform before his eyes, like the monster Edward Hyde turning back into the kind Doctor Henry Jeckyll. "She needs a friend right now — someone who is not too close and not too distant, but who can be objective."

"Got it."

That night, a broken Kerry Noland found a getaway in a tiny rat-hole of a bar downtown named, "Jake's Place." It was the only establishment open, besides the Quick Stop, so she pulled into the rock-strewn parking lot. Concrete block walls couldn't contain the reverberation of the bass inside. Nor could they keep her wounded soul out. Neon lights spelling the names of various brands of beer hung from seventies-era wallboard, gold globe lights dangled from chains over four booths, and a small TV broadcast a national basketball game behind the bar.

Before Jake poured her third Vodka, they found her. Using one pick-up line after another, the three men, stinking of dirt and sweat, fawned over her. To them she was fresh meat — something as rare as a box of gold in Fair Hope. But to Kerry, she was less than dirt. She didn't care.

After the fifth drink, she rose from the bar stool, grabbed the grungy hand of the ugliest of the three and guided him, winding, to the door and outside. The others followed like mutts chasing a bone.

In the parking lot, her back against the bar wall, the disgusting man pushed his weight on her as his drinking buddies cheered him on. The cheering stopped when a short, skinny man stepped out of the shadows and slid a shiny blade against the base of the man's throat. "Fun's over, boys," he said. "Time to move on."

One of the men took a step in his direction. "You're all by yourself, old man. You can't stop all three of us."

"You wanna try?" the old man said. "I brought back plenty hurt and hate from 'Nam to take out two of ya before the third even knows it. Now back away and we'll call it even. You can go back inside and lie to Jake about the great time you had with Miss Noland."

Kerry's eyes grew wide and she leaned her head to identify the man, but the booze, the darkness, the guilt was too thick to allow her to see clearly.

Both men stared at the tattoo on the old guy's arm and inched away. He pushed the big guy off Kerry and toward his friends. "You can have her," the ugly man said. "She's just a skank anyhow."

Kerry, once proud corporate executive of a billion dollar company, slid down the gritty concrete block wall to the jagged rocks of the parking lot where she gave in to the darkness. Rough hands grabbed her arms and pulled her up from the gravel.

The man's skinny hand pressed her chest, pushing her back onto the bare wall while the other dragged open her purse and dug through its contents. The man found the keys to her car and pulled her towards it. Lights flashed inside — he'd unlocked the doors, and she was pushed into the back seat. An old beach towel, taken from her trunk, was draped over her body like a funeral pall.

The man opened the driver's door and the engine roared to life. Kerry watched flashes of light zip by one by one, through the moon roof of the car. Their monotonous display, along with the steady hum of the engine, hypnotized her into a shallow sleep. She awoke for a moment when the driver lugged her into a dark room and lay her on a bed. "Here it comes," she thought through the haze, but the sound of the slamming of a huge metal door told her the worse was over. She grasped a pillow and pulled it to her stomach. Hugging it tight, she fell asleep.

CHAPTER FIFTEEN

"I ain't got nowhere else to go," Sheryl shouted at the man standing inside the doorway of the insurance company office. She'd stayed there the night before, as she had many other times. It wasn't the best place in the city. It was cramped and when cold winds and rain blew, it didn't offer much cover. But the better places, like the overpass on Independence or the front of the library, were already taken.

When the owner had seen her through the plate glass window, a clear wall to keep her out and to keep him in, his face turned beet red and his eyes burned like fireballs. He shoved the door open and yelled, "Get the hell out of here!"

Everybody knew he and other store owners had pushed the city to move homeless people away — make them somebody else's problem. In response, Sheryl and her friends learned to be invisible. Slip in well after dark, get rest, and then go away before the store opened. "You all closed down the shelter on MLK, and I gotta sleep somewhere. You tell me to go there. They tell me to come here."

"Sleep anywhere else," he said. "You scare away customers and smell up the doorway. You're killing my business."

"Well, maybe you should take your damn business someplace else 'stead of making me sleep someplace else."

"I'm gonna call the cops."

She knew the routine. "Call 'em. They know me. We're on a first name basis." She stood up tall, as tall as a short woman could stand, and watched as the man closed and locked the door before going to an office in the back. Leaning over, she picked up her bag of stuff and shuffled up the street. She was tired of the way she'd been pushed around and threatened by rich snobs who thought they were better than she was. They didn't understand how tough things had been — how she'd lost Danielle, and lost her money to her lazy ex-husband, and lost her home to the bank. They sat in their homes — big, fancy houses, watching big, fancy TVs and eating big, fancy meals with their big, fat families, while she and her friends struggled to find a place to sleep and something to eat. It was hard — real hard. Harder when it got cold. And it had been like this for three years. Three years without a home, without money, without her daughter.

Danielle. Sheryl used to think about her every night before she fell asleep. She had been a beautiful young girl, filled with a bright spirit. Everybody loved being around her. But she also had a rebellious streak. Her father, drunk half the time and angry the rest, had a bad habit of criticizing everything Sheryl and Danielle did. Sometimes he let his fists do the talking. It wasn't no surprise when, at fourteen, Danielle hooked up with a no-good redneck, the mirror image of her father. Three weeks later, she had disappeared.

At first Sheryl spent every waking minute walking the streets of Charlotte and questioning people as she searched for Danielle. A kid her age said she'd gone south — to Florida or Alabama or someplace warm. An old drunk said he'd seen her in a crack house up town. One old lady said she was a prostitute in Atlanta. Kids these days, especially if they had a father like Danielle's, did real stupid stuff.

But Sheryl never found her. Her search took a toll. She worked at a little dingy fast-food restaurant when she wasn't looking for Danielle, but she didn't make enough to keep her head above water. Naturally, her man did nothing to help. He stayed drunk, Danielle never came home, and the bank took her house. When the manager of the restaurant where she worked found out she was homeless, he fired her on the spot, saying she wasn't reliable anymore. It's hard to be reliable when you ain't got nowhere to live.

Sheryl fought her way back. She learned to play the homeless game, found out how to get help, landed temporary work here and there, and was finally climbing out of the hole. She did it all for the baby in her belly. Just a little longer and she'd be able to get a steady place to live and a job. Just a little longer.

She knew the Charlotte Police would come around to bother her, but she didn't expect they would get there so soon. The patrol car pulled to the curb and the window rolled down. "Shirley? Shirley!"

She stopped, her shoulders slumped, and she turned to face the cop in the car. "It's Sheryl."

"We received a report you were loitering in one of the business doorways."

"I weren't loitering. I was resting."

"You know you can't sleep in front of these stores, right?"

"Yeah. You told me that before." She couldn't count the times.

"So why are you still here?"

"Guess I ain't got nowhere else to go."

"You can go to the shelter on Tryon."

"They got a four night a month limit."

"What about the others?"

"They fill up fast."

"Well, you can't stay here."

"All right." She turned to walk away.

"I'm serious, Shirley."

"So am I," she mumbled and leaned into the wind. "And, it's Sheryl."

When Kerry awoke, she surveyed the strange bedroom — the box shelf, jutting out between two beds on which sat an alarm clock, a phone, and an over-sized, hideous-looking lamp. Memories of the horrible experience from the night before threatened to consume her, but she pushed each thought back down, shielding herself from the horrors of the night, stopped when a man intervened and brought her here.

Startled, she sat up and searched the room. She was alone. Her purse was on the end table. A quick look inside assured her that nothing was missing, at least from what she could tell. The alarm clock indicated it was two o'clock in the afternoon, but surely she couldn't have slept that long. The settings must have been wrong. She stumbled outside in the harsh afternoon sunlight — the clock was right after all — and retrieved the small travel bag from her car. In the shower she scrubbed hard to remove the grit from the close encounter in the parking lot, wincing when she touched the bruises on her arms and flinching when the hot water scalded the deep scratches on her back. But it couldn't cleanse her soul.

Then the tears. Sitting on the edge of the tub, wrapped in a small bath towel from the rack above, Kerry cried long and hard. She wept from a sense of guilt and worthlessness. She bawled for seeking the abuse that almost happened in the parking lot. She sobbed for Todd Sanders. Then she returned to the shower and stayed there long after the water turned from scalding to freezing, wishing to wash away the pain, the guilt.

She packed her things and drove the short distance to the motel office and asked the man at the counter if he could tell her how she came to be staying in that hotel. In a slow, southern, country boy dialect he told her a skinny runt of a man, long white beard beneath his chin, had checked into that room. "Seen him hitch-hiking on '76 once or twice, but I don't know who he is."

She had turned to walk away when he added, "He had a picture of a flag hanging from a rifle tattooed on his arm. Guess he was in the army, but it must have been a long time ago."

The motel was in Chadbourn, about fifteen miles away from Fair Hope. On the way back home, Kerry scanned the road for the skinny man with the army tattoo. She found him sitting on a bench facing an empty children's playground on Felton Street. "Howdy, Ma'am," he said as she approached.

"It was you," she announced.

"I ain't done nothing."

Kerry stood before him like an accuser. "Who are you?" she demanded.

"Eugene," he said. "But you can call me Gene."

She relaxed her shoulders just a bit. "You saved my life."

The skinny man rubbed dingy fingers through his dirty beard. "Don't believe I've heard anyone say those words in a long time."

"Last night. At the bar. You saved me from those men and took me to the motel in Chadbourn."

He patted the bench beside him. "Maybe I did, maybe I didn't."

His elusiveness irritated the once Type A businesswoman. She tried to see beyond the beard, wrinkles, and scars, for a reason a stranger —

someone who didn't know her — would be her rescuer. She saw insecurities and fears, buoyed by hope and wounds and pain, and tempered by... compassion.

"But you're just a homeless man. Why would you help me?" At this point, why would anyone help her?

"Maybe I know some things you don't, Kerry."

"How did you know my name?"

"Don't ever-one in Charlotte know Miss Kerry Noland, CEO of Bell Intelliservices?"

She gazed out past the playground to a field of dandelions, white spheres that should be blown away by little children.

"Dandelions are pretty this time of year," he said. In his hand he held the stalk of one, the fluffy white crown undulating in the light breeze, threatening to blow away. He handed it to her.

"Do you live in Charlotte?"

"I've lived all over this state... in other states, too... and in other countries — Vietnam, fer instance."

Hazy memories of words from the night before washed through her mind. With a manicured fingernail, she scratched old and cracked paint from the bench where she sat. An obnoxious smell of decaying garbage drifted from a dented garbage can a few feet away and she welcomed it. A car drove by, bass blasting so hard she could feel it, and for once, she didn't curse the car's driver. She had time, all the time in the world, for the important things. No board meetings, no phone calls, no demanding employees, but the precious sense that what she needed right then was the ability to just... be. And she welcomed it.

"My daddy fought in Vietnam. When were you there?" she asked.

"Back in seventy... seventy-one. Two tours." He rubbed both hands up and down his cheeks above his gray beard. "What branch? Your daddy."

"Army, I think. Only one tour. But then, the newspaper said he was in the 101st Airborne Division. Is that the Air Force?"

The old man turned to face her. "101st? The Screaming Eagles?"

"That's what the paper said. Why?"

"They were real heroes... one of the toughest outfits in the army. Have been since World War II. Still are."

"That can't be... My father was never a hero."

"Maybe he was before you knew him..."

"What?"

His eyes locked hers and his voice softened to a hoarse whisper. "When you're in a war, fear burnin' through your veins, fire and explosions all around you, your buddies dying in your arms... that changes things." His eyes glazed over. Turning, he stared ahead, at the playground and the park. "The Screamin' Eagles were paratroopers... a bunch of tough mothers the army set up to fight in enemy territory. Viet Cong called the Screamin' Eagles the Chicken Men 'cause they had never seen an eagle, not to mention a screaming one. And they were all scared of 'em."

"I had no idea."

"Yeah. Some pretty famous sons-of-bitches were Screamin' Eagles. Bob Kalsu — Rookie of the year for the Buffalo Bills — for one. He died over in 'Nam. Jimi Hendrix — yeah, he was an Eagle in the early sixties." He leaned back on the bench, soaking in the sun and the memory. "Purple Haze all in my brain... Hee-hee. Yeah, they were bad." Gene blinked his eyes. "When?"

"When? When was he in the army? I don't know. About 1969, '70, I think."

"Holy..." He turned back toward her. "He must have been in Ripcord in seventy."

"Fire Support Base Ripcord? I read that in the paper. He was a sergeant. So why is that important?"

Eugene shook his head. "That battle was as ugly as they come. Worse than Hamburger Hill. Worse than Tet. Your daddy was a sergeant? My Lord. They called 'em 'Shake 'n Bake' back then 'cause they were thrown into command so goddam quick — had no training, no experience. Didn't get any respect. Couldn't do much good."

Kerry pondered his words. Her father. Too young and inexperienced for leadership and thrown into hell, discarded with the other rubbish.

"Ripcord. Supposed to stop Charlie on the Ho Chi Minh trail, but the chiefs took so long to plan it, everyone in North Vietnam, from Hanoi to Ha Giang knew about it. And they were ready. Army was outnumbered 'bout ten to one. In three weeks in July, seventy-five American soldiers were killed and about four hundred were wounded. If your daddy was in Ripcord, he was lucky to come out alive."

Tears filled her eyes.

"He did survive, didn't he?"

She nodded. "But he shot himself a few years after he came home."

"Ain't no surprise there. Horrible times." Eugene's eyes narrowed as he turned again to face her. "I don't care who he was. Anyone who fought in Project Fire Support Base Ripcord struggled after he returned home. They didn't call it PTSD back then, but hauntin' horrors chased all of us. That place was Hell, and when you been to Hell, you're gonna bring back some demons."

She leaned against the back of the bench, caught her breath and whispered, "I had no idea..."

"Of course, you didn't. You weren't there. Neither were the rest of the people living in America. They had no idea. Still don't. That sorta thing will change a man forever — always for the worse."

"I never knew my father."

"But he knew you. Count on that." A broad smile filled his face. "But then, I may be wrong. I'm just an old homeless guy with no place to go... 'cause I ain't got a home. Get it?" He stood, grabbed a small backpack beside him, and turned back toward town. "Wherever it is, I better be getting there, right?"

"Wait!" She opened her purse. "What do I owe you?"

"Huh? Nothing. I paid for your room with your own money from your handbag." He tapped his temple, gave a wink, and turned to leave while she stared at the bottom of her purse.

Raising her head, she called, "Do you need a ride?"

"Nope."

"Thank you," she called after the odd little man.

He just waved and walked on down the road. "'I gotta ramble, woa, woa, I gotta move on, woa, woa, I gotta walk away my blues.' We Five, 1966. Hee-hee."

Kerry gazed down at the dandelion in her hands. The seed head was gone, leaving the naked stalk alone in her fingers. When she looked up, Gene had gone.

CHAPTER SIXTEEN

To reach Fair Hope Cemetery, Kerry drove down Main Street and veered right onto Johnston Road. On the outskirts of Fair Hope, located in a large, open piece of sandy soil peeking through tufts of grass and scattered oaks, headstones jutted skyward, monuments of famous, and infamous, ancestors. She hesitated after pressing the "Off" button in her Lexus. She wanted to find Jack (JC) Noland's grave, and she didn't want to at the same time. But she knew this was part of her journey, a step she had to take or the quest would be for naught. In the far corner, at the end of a grown over drive, almost reaching the tree line between the cemetery and Johnston Road, she found it. The small monument at the head of the gravesite listed his name and the dates: Born: 1951, Died: 1977. Above the inscription was the image of a chevron containing the head of an eagle and the esteemed inscription, "Screaming Eagles, 101st Airborne Division." The ground around the grave was void of flowers. Weeds threatened to overtake the clumpy fescue grass.

Hands folded in reverence, Kerry stood before her father's tiny monument. He deserved a better one — much larger and much more impressive. This was her daddy — a man she once saw as a miserable failure, but now a real hero who had endured the horrors of battle and the demons that followed as long as he could. Now she knew. She was wrong to blame him for failing to succeed. She was wrong to hate him. She was wrong... for turning that hatred in to herself. She had made mistakes — terrible ones.

The pain in her heart grew into a stabbing pain and she fell to her knees. She grabbed her side to hold off the torment, but the effort failed.

Tears of exhaustion, torment, and agony made her cry as she had seldom cried before.

Within several excruciating minutes the agony subsided and she rose to leave. But not before whispering, "I do love you, Daddy." Daddy — she had never called her father, "Daddy."

On her way out of town, she stopped by Grishom's Funeral Home and ordered a new headstone for Jack (JC) Noland's grave. "This is a mighty fine thing for you to do, Miss Noland," the tall black-suited director of the facility said. "We'll take care of it right away."

She also visited the mayor's office, introduced herself and wrote a large check to help recognize Jack Noland and rebuild Fair Hope. She could tell the town needed millions but her gift was a start. She also promised to help persuade state and federal politicians to release emergency relief aid for the community. The mayor's mouth turned from a congenial smile to a beaming grin. "Why, Miss Noland. I thank you," he said when he studied the check. "I'll ensure that we do everything we can to help the community know and revere Jack's service." He studied the check again, as if to be sure it was legitimate. "I knew Jack. We went to high school together. He was a year or so older than I."

"What do you remember about my father?"

"Jack was a good man... an excellent man. First string tight end on the football team. If anyone was destined to be successful, it was Jack Noland. Then the war got him. He was so proud to serve his country, but when he returned from 'Nam, he suffered some terrible trauma. It drove him mad. He couldn't focus, couldn't work, couldn't keep a job. I tried to help him get work as a mechanic at Roy's Auto Repair, but he didn't show up for work on the first day. The war destroyed him, like it destroyed so many other boys who served back then. Cryin' shame."

Kerry pushed back the tears forming in her eyes. How she wished she had known her father when he had hope and promise. How she wished she had not been so ready to judge him after his Vietnam experience.

"Then, when he... passed, we were all so sad. He was broke. The town was struggling, but somehow we raised enough to pay for his plot out in Powell Cemetery. That was the least we could do, but all we could do. But now, with your helpful support, we'll be able to recognize him for the hero he was."

Kerry stood to leave. She had heard what she needed to know.

"I should add, this donation will go so far to help our town live up to the beauty of its name — Fair Hope," he stared up at the ceiling — the consummate politician — proud of his profound comment.

Kerry stopped. She turned and said, "I beg your pardon?"

"We have a rich history in these parts that was almost lost in the recent storms. Matthew and Florence devastated our lovely city. But we will come back. In time, Fair Hope *will* live up to its name."

"I never thought Fair Hope had much history."

"Oh, yes, she does. I've been trying to get that word out for years." He leaned forward, a professor preparing to deliver a lecture and Kerry listened carefully. "There are actually two stories about the founding of this town."

Kerry ignored the clock on the mayor's desk when it chimed five o'clock. So did the mayor.

"Both stories date back to the early 1800s. A struggling businessman named William Radcliff — he was my great, great, grandpa, on my mama's side — couldn't make a dime out of a dollar, but he kept trying. Word was he was an easy target and people around the state took advantage of him. Folks called him 'Hopeless Bill,' 'cause he failed again and again. But he gave it one more shot. He thought this part of the state needed a trading store, and he might have a fair shake at success, so he built the first one here. Named it, 'Fair Hope Traders'. Eventually convinced the townsfolk to name the community Fair Hope and he became the first mayor. The rest is, as they say, history."

So Fair Hope was a turn-around town.

His eyes sparkled. "But I like the second story best. Seems Mr. Radcliff wasn't such a bad egg after all. In fact, his store was successful and he gained a reputation around the state. On one trip to Raleigh, he fell in love with a woman of means named Isabella Hope. She seldom ventured outdoors like the laborers, so she had the fairest skin. You know where I'm goin," he said with a gleam and a grin. "To woo her to the area and to his heart, he worked to name the town Fair Hope. She married him and the town grew into a successful stopping place between Charlotte and the beaches to the south. The rest is good ole' history." He beamed a smile, proud of his knowledge.

On her way home to Charlotte, Kerry's thoughts were on her father, the hero who never was able to fulfill his purpose, the tiny town she now so proudly called home, and her responsibilities back in Charlotte.

• • •

It was rare for Angela to pick Emma up from school — she was usually working the evening shift. With their busy schedules, it was even more rare for the two of them to commit time to being together. Usually, Emma would do homework and Angela would pay bills, cook, or straighten up around the house. But these were unusual times that required special measures. Angela only hoped she wasn't too late. So, after school, she and Emma took a walk through a neighborhood park with trails that wound through woods beside a large lake. Spring rains had coaxed colors in the leaves, and the ground was muddy and marshy. Crickets chirped nosily along the grassy shores and a hoot owl could be heard high in the trees.

"I'm real concerned that you're okay, kiddo," Angela said, with a bit of a tremble in her voice. "How do you like Dr. Marks-Thompson?" Her heart pounded as she hoped her daughter would feel comfortable enough to share her honest thoughts.

"She's real nice, Mom. Easy to talk to." Songbirds, on their way back up north after the winter, stationed themselves in trees overhead as the two walked the trails. "Have you talked to Dad?" Emma asked, almost a whisper.

"No. I have an appointment with an attorney day after tomorrow, and she says it would be better if all communication went through her."

"What does that mean?"

"I imagine she will file a restraining order pretty soon. In the meantime, we'll tell your father you are either sick or busy this weekend. You won't have to go to his house again." She draped her arm across Emma's shoulder, pulling her closer. "We will get through this. I promise."

Emma bit her lip. "Will dad get mad at me?"

"I don't know. I'm sure he will be angry with me. Count on that."

"I don't want to cause trouble."

Her words melted Angela's aching heart. "You aren't causing trouble, sweetie. Your father did."

Emma hugged her mother tight. Angela relished the gesture. One thing that was coming out of this nightmare was a drastic improvement in their relationship. That was good.

———— • ————

Jim's conversation with Gene at the homeless shelter haunted him, but it didn't stop him from volunteering there. He spent up to three nights a week. But that didn't occupy all his time nor did he feel it made the best use of his skills and resources. So, he made financial donations to the YMCA, the American Cancer Society, and a local charity for stroke victims. But he still felt like he could do more.

One afternoon while checking his mail, he found a fund-raising letter from an obscure, nonprofit called King's Kare. After tossing the brochure into the trash, he thought how odd it was to name an organization in Charlotte — The Queen City — King's Kare. Intrigued, he retrieved the envelope and examined its contents.

The material inside offended the marketer in him. "Meet Our Clients And There Support Animals," the title, printed in large, bright pink Comic Sans font jumped out from the top of the page. Two pages of bright red text, full of misspellings and run-on sentences, followed. A third page, just of photos of people with various dogs, rounded out the letter. Finally, as if to damn the fund raiser to certain failure, a return envelope, without postage, was tucked inside. It was an example of everything wrong to do in a marketing letter. Irritated that someone would dare request funding in such a pitiful manner, he picked up his phone and dialed the number, only half visible due to margin errors, in the footer.

"Hello?"

"Who is this?" Jim demanded more than asked.

"Beverly. Who's this?"

So, Beverly has no last name. "I'm calling about the charity letter I received this afternoon. Do you know anything about this?"

"Oh, King's Kare. I'm the president and founder. Would you like to make a donation? We take all major credit cards."

Jim pulled the phone from his ear and stared at it, amazed he had just heard a request for money. He returned the phone to his ear and said, "Is this legitimate?" No sooner than he said it then he realized it was a stupid thing to ask since no one would actually admit their fund raising scam was not above board, but he was amazed at the incompetence and the audacity of the "president and founder" of King's Kare.

"Let me tell you our story," Beverly said. Then, with a sweet, southern drawl, she described how she and her late husband had started the organization over ten years ago when they discovered their sweet, mixed-breed dog named King had an amazing impact on the personality and behavior of William, their grandson, who had been diagnosed with an Anankastic behavior disorder.

The woman was so different from the brochure. She was engaging and compassionate. And she knew her stuff. Obviously, she had told her story before. She said that the disorder was known as an obsessive-compulsive disorder and that it resulted in poor social skills for the victims. Those at the farthest end of the spectrum could not function in society. William wasn't that extreme, but his disorder did affect his interactions with others, and his behavior improved whenever their dog was present. He and the dog became best friends, and William seemed to become more sociable. After King passed away, they introduced more "therapy dogs" to aid him, and branched out to serve others in the local community, with a good deal of success.

In a flash, the message made sense to Jim. He had often wondered if his brother suffered from some sort of borderline obsessive-compulsive disorder. David's rigid behavior and his weak social skills suggested it, but he had never been formally diagnosed. Perhaps a dog, like those with Beverly's organization, would have helped him when he was younger.

"So would you like to help support us?" Beverly asked. Sweet, simple.

Jim examined the photos from the mailer again. Dogs of all shapes and sizes with happy people in a variety of settings — work, playground, fishing, classroom, bedroom. Convinced by Beverly's sales pitch and out of concern for people like David, Jim said he'd like to learn more and scheduled an appointment that afternoon at her business.

Beverly met him on the porch of her small farmhouse outside Mint Hill and welcomed him inside. She was diminutive next to Jim. She wore a flowing, flowery blouse and white shorts that came to her knees, the kind of outfit a lady twenty years older than Jim might wear.

As he walked through the front door, Jim was accosted by half a dozen dogs that nuzzled and drooled on him. The King's Kare humble office was Beverly's kitchen table. With all the pride of a successful entrepreneur, Beverly described again the wonderful service her dogs provided to people with Anankastic disorders. She showed a photo of her now-grown grandson with a large, furry mutt in an office cubicle, grinning a smile only the happy, satisfied could display. "He's working in Raleigh now, with Queenie, his support dog."

Jim took in the photograph. "Beverly, I think King's Kare is a wonderful service, and I want to help," Jim said. "Maybe with a financial gift, but we can talk about that later."

"Oh?"

"If you'll allow me to, I'd like to offer some professional support."

Beverly frowned.

"Now, hear me out," Jim said. "I have over forty years of business marketing experience, most recently with Bell Intelliservices."

"That's a big organization."

"True," he said. "But marketing is marketing, and the principles that made Bell successful can also help you get the word out about King's Kare. That is, if you'll let me."

"I'm afraid I couldn't afford you."

"I'm not looking for money, and frankly I don't want any. I offer my marketing services to your organization, as my gift, for free."

"I don't understand," Beverly said.

"Here is what I propose. One afternoon every other week I would like to visit your office to help prepare fund raising mailers, publicity materials, and tracking tools. I believe I can improve your response rate and raise your proceeds. And again, this will be at no charge to you or your organization."

She frowned again and turned her gaze to the photograph of her son and his dog.

"I want to help in this way because I believe what I can do for you in terms of marketing can be much more valuable than a simple donation." He leaned forward and said, "What do you think?"

She looked back to him, exploring his eyes as if to determine his sincerity. "Welcome aboard, Mr. Bishop," she said, extending her hand.

"Jim. Call me Jim... boss."

She matched his smile with hers.

As he drove away, Jim determined his intention, unlike his volunteer service at the shelter, was truly altruistic. He didn't expect to receive anything in return. It was something he could do, he was skilled at it, so he agreed to do it.

It was good to be back at Bell. While the office trappings — the carpet, window treatments, and furniture — had been replaced in a makeover two years earlier, Kerry felt the office carried a sense of newness, representing a profound new start.

She called in the CFO, the HR Director, and the Marketing Director. The finance guy was dressed in a conservative, dark suit with a light blue shirt and red tie. The head of HR wore a brown jacket and yellow shirt without a tie. The Director of Marketing was decked out in his traditional three-piece suit, a tie that appeared to have been painted by Jackson Pollock, and gleaming loafers. Images of the Three Musketeers, the Three Stooges, the Three Amigos, all flashed in her head and she had to stifle a snide remark and a laugh. They all looked like they had been called on the carpet. "Relax, guys," Kerry said. "You've done nothing wrong."

They still looked tense. The head of HR jotted in his notebook.

"I've been thinking about how we can be better perceived in our city. We haven't put a lot of effort into community involvement in the past, and I think we have a lot of room for improvement. One of the things we can do is to set aside funds to support veterans."

The CFO said, "I don't know where we are going to find the money to..."

"Start with the contingency funds in my budget. Let me know how much you think we can spend from that line item immediately. Next year we'll find ways to increase it."

The CFO sat back, silent.

"While we're talking about funds, I want to set up a matching funds system to support a local suicide prevention organization in Todd Sanders' name. I will personally donate the first $50,000."

"Well," the CFO said, "since that won't affect the budget, I see no reason not to."

Kerry turned to the director of HR. "I would like you to set up a series of required courses on suicide prevention and communication. In addition, let's explore best practices in employee stress management techniques and convey those to management."

The HR guy wrote frantically in his notebook. He made no mention that he had proposed the stress management idea two years earlier, but Kerry knew it was on his mind. She had ignored it at the time.

To the director of marketing she said, "It's important for you to get the word out to the community that we are taking these initiatives, okay?"

"I'll draft some press releases and get them to you by this..."

"I don't need to see them," she said. "I trust you to manage that."

His mouth dropped.

With their orders intact, the three men marched out of her office in single file.

Just before noon, her assistant knocked on her door and asked if she could come in. Kerry's immediate staff had come and gone so quickly over the years that she realized she had known little about any of them. The younger woman entered the office and Kerry said, "I don't believe I've ever asked you what name you'd prefer I call you."

"Alissa. My first name."

"Good, Alissa. How can I help you?"

"Uh, did you have a good time off, ma'am?"

"It was very beneficial. All in all, yes."

Alissa acted sheepish — guarded.

"Is there something else, Alissa?"

"Well, rumors are out that something different's going on... Are you okay?"

Kerry couldn't have hid her smile if she'd wanted to. "I'm fine. Thank you for asking. And I'm glad to hear about the rumors. They say, most rumors contain at least a bit of truth." She winked as she said it. "You know," she added, "we should go to lunch this week to get to know each other better."

"Yes, ma'am," Alissa said, looking much like the three men who had just left.

"Nothing's wrong," Kerry said. "Just girl chat. Would you put that on our schedules?"

Alissa nodded and turned toward the exit.

"Oh, and Alissa... Would you contact Jim Bishop?" Kerry asked. "He used to work here. A couple of weeks ago he came by, asking for a donation to a local homeless shelter. Call him and ask him to come see me about how we can help, okay?"

Alissa's eyes grew wide. No doubt she recalled Kerry's last meeting with Bishop... one that didn't turn out so well. When she reached her desk, she picked up her phone and dialed an extension number. Kerry smiled to herself, again. *Go ahead. Spread the word. A new, kinder, gentler sheriff is in town.*

• • •

Evan Griffen's dentist office address was easy to find. A quick search online and information popped up like magic. The website indicated it closed at 6:00, but with a little luck, Evan might not leave until about 6:30 — dusk for this time of year in Charlotte — the perfect time of day. So now, it was time to wait. His gut told him he was making the right decision, but his heart wasn't so sure. He chose to follow his gut.

He backed his aging car into a space in the rear of the parking lot and surveilled the area. A light rain, typical for Charlotte, made it hard to view the complex. The long, low building housed a variety of shops and offices, each with a backdoor exiting into the parking lot. Two flowerpots stood like sentries on either side of the doorways. In the dimming afternoon light and hazy drizzle, he could make out purple flowers sitting atop green masts in each planter. His wife had planted some — he thought she'd called them Grape Hyacinths — last fall. Evan's new red Corvette was in the space in front of the rear door to his office. Security cameras were strategically located to cover most of the area, as would be expected in an upscale shopping center. Trees covered a few sections, but their spring buds offered little cover from the cameras. He was about to abandon his plans when he noticed the little alcoves covering the exit doors of each office provided some privacy, except for the ceiling lights above each. Now the issue was how to be at those back doors without the office staff noticing.

He pulled out of the parking lot and onto the street out of view of the cameras, and then called Evan's office and received a voice mail message, "... Our office is now closed. If this is an emergency..."

Since the Corvette was still parked outside the office door, Evan was probably just preparing to leave. It was time. Stepping from his car into the rain, he wrapped himself in a long trench coat. That and the rain would help keep his identity secret. He tugged the collar up — like the undercover detectives did in old detective movies — and approached the back of the building. He slinked up beside the Vette and into the alcove. It took a minute to stretch up and remove the globe fixture to expose the single light bulb. His heart pounded.

Through the heavy exit door, he could hear voices inside. One sounded male. A moment later, the handle twisted and an umbrella, still closed, pointed the way into the darkness. He reached up and slapped the light bulb and the hallway became dark. The door opened wider and Evan's head appeared. He looked up to the ceiling where the globe had been, closed the door behind him, and the alcove became dark.

The first punch to his jaw flung him back against the brick wall with almost enough force to alert the office staff inside. Evan was tall, but flabby, and the blow sank a bit into his cheek. He would bruise easily. The second punch, to his midriff, doubled him over. A third glanced off Evan's face, scraping bare knuckles against the rough brick wall. Three pile-driver pounds to his head dropped him to his hands and knees.

"What do you want?" Evan mumbled without raising his head.

The man leaned down and whispered next to Evan's ear. "You need to learn respect — respect for your family — respect for Emma."

At the sound of her name, Evan swept his hand out, trying to knock him off his feet, but he missed. "Leave her alone."

A sharp kick to his solar plexus knocked the wind out of him, silencing him again. "*You* leave her alone," he whispered, followed by two deadly punches to Evan's lower back.

Evan's head hung even lower beneath his shoulders.

"Your coaching days are over. If you ever do anything to hurt Emma again, if you touch her, we'll have another talk. And it will be your last." A kick to his gut jerked him off the concrete stoop and down to his belly in a crushed mass of bruised flesh. To seal the deal, the man stomped on the fingers of Evan's right hand, suspending his dental practice for a long time.

Evan's position — crumpled, writhing, and whimpering — provided enough time to hurry to the street where the aging car waited, and drive away. While streetlights flashed by overhead, Rev. Allen Rhodes, three-times Golden Globes Champion, brought his battered hand to his lips and sucked the blood from his broken flesh.

CHAPTER SEVENTEEN

Kerry got to work and called a meeting of the Board of Bell Intelliservices. Made up of five men and one woman, all CEOs in the tech community, the board had exercised its power with little regard for little people. Acquisitions, layoffs, and bonuses were decided with only the bottom line in mind. She had created the board in her own image. She used to like it that way.

But it was time for a makeover.

Following the expected greetings and spoken concerns about her health, she rose to address the group. Each member sat stoically around the table. Word had gotten out that Kerry was making changes, and the Board was tentative. Alissa passed out folders to each member as Kerry stood to speak. "After considerable thought, I have concluded that Bell Intelliservices can be a much bigger and better force in our industry and in our community. We face some serious issues, but they are not insurmountable obstacles. I am prepared to discuss the recommendations — as outlined in your folders for as long as necessary, and will call for a vote on each by the end of our meeting."

Everyone browsed through their folders.

"First, I want to add two more positions to the Board, preferably for female executives in the tech industry." Several men in the group frowned. One rolled his eyes. She had expected this response. "I'd like to make this a major agenda item at our next meeting."

"What is this second point," the Chairman of the Board asked, "under Employee Relations Improvements? I thought we had some of the best employees in Charlotte."

"We do... But we also have some of the highest turnover rates in Charlotte," Kerry said. "I believe that stems from the way we've treated our people in the past. I admit that I have played a major role in causing employee issues and I am ready to help make things right. But I also want us to address this on a corporate level."

The chairman sat back.

"I asked Human Resources to study this, to explore best practices in other companies, and to come up with a multi-faceted approach to making Bell a more employee-supportive place to work."

Grumbling rose from all six board members. The Chairman raised his Mont Blanc off the desk, a sign he wanted to ask another question. "Ms. Noland..."

When the chairman addressed her as, "Ms. Noland," Kerry knew the battle lines were being drawn.

"How much will this cost?"

"The cost will be minimal. Most of these improvements can be done in-house with little impact on our budget. Some expense will be incurred, and I expect HR will detail those for us in upcoming board meetings.

"In addition to my direction to HR about this issue, I insist that our organization initiate an assistance program for people with depression, especially for those who struggle with thoughts of suicide. We should implement a matching fundraising campaign, and I will submit the first fifty thousand dollars, to help our employees. Management training to recognize such issues, an internal suicide hotline, and beefed-up counseling services in Employee Relations, all should be parts of our effort."

That one was difficult to argue with and most of the Board members nodded... although begrudgingly. The reticent response reaffirmed her thoughts. The board members would be hesitant to support change and her recommendations would be met with resistance. But she felt strongly about the ideas, about the opportunities she was proposing, and she had no choice but to make her case. The next item would be the hardest...

"Another concern, in my opinion, regards our presence in the cities in which we have call centers. We need to improve our reputation in our communities. We've been seen as an organization that helps only those who help us — a quid-pro-quo arrangement — but does little for the true needs for those around us. I recommend we work to improve our image immediately. And, this will require a little financial input."

Three board members sat back with arms crossed. Two others sat up straight, another sign of defiance.

"As you know, Charlotte, like every large city, has a homeless problem. That also goes for Cleveland, Lubbock, and Seattle, where we have satellite operations. A lot of talk, but little real action has circulated among our community leaders. I recommend we take immediate steps to help the homeless, first here in Charlotte, home to our headquarters, and later in the other cities in which we have a major presence. I want us to repurpose the offices in the southern part of our first floor, which is primarily storage right now, into apartment housing for select homeless women and children."

"Now hold on there," one of the long-term board members said.

"They will have their own entrance, so they can come and go without notice, and without affecting our work. Their apartments will have full facilities — kitchens, bathrooms, bedrooms, and Bell will cover the utilities."

"This seems so sudden. I'm not so sure we should incur such expenses willy-nilly. It may be detrimental to our bottom line," the Chairman said.

"This is something that our city needs and that we can do, and the benefits far outweigh the cost," Kerry said.

"Shouldn't we take a little more time... Maybe hire an outside firm to do a feasibility study..."

"The time for waiting has passed, and as far as feasibility, I think you'll agree this is within our grasp. We can hire one or more employees to help manage this facility, so Bell will be completely hands-off. This person can also work with local search agencies to help residents find good jobs and become productive citizens."

"Ms. Noland..." another board member said.

"I don't intend to go this alone. I'm sure we can find local grants from Charlotte, Mecklenberg county, and civic support organizations. In addition, I'd like to challenge other organizations that have a major stake in North Carolina to match our efforts. Some of them have spotty reputations these days and we can help them improve their image. Bank of America, BB&T, and Wells Fargo would be interested, I'm sure. Lowes would be willing to donate materials. Duke Energy, Hanes, Nucor... They, too, would surely enjoy the positive press such an endeavor would bring."

The chairman interrupted again. "Aren't you concerned about how such initiatives will impact our organization?"

"That is precisely what I want to happen," Kerry said. "I want to impact our organization and our community. I want to set an example and I believe we are well suited to do just that. This won't end the homeless problem on our city, but it will be a good start and a strong model for others to follow."

The battle had just begun, but she believed it was a battle she could win. She figured she'd just put it out there. "I recommend our first steps, and our initial investment, be to give half a million dollars over the next five years from our community support fund to establish our in-house residence facility. In addition, I'd like to donate a hundred thousand to the Charlotte Homeless Shelter to help support their efforts." Grumbling filled the room.

The gauntlet thrown, Kerry leaned on the podium. "Now, what are your questions?"

Trees in the courtyard, naked of leaves since the fall, reached out thick branches and tiny, spiny limbs, like demons stretching toward employees leaving the building. Sunlight showed through the limbs and made dark lines, spider legs, on the white sidewalk.

Sheryl was usually in the food line at the community center, bundled in her protective sweatshirt, at this time of the day. But she had something important to do.

She stood on the side of the little break area at the employee entrance to Bell Intelliservices. People were coming out for lunch, walking up the street to restaurants she couldn't hope to go into or to the food truck parked by the curb, where the guy inside ignored her.

Sheryl didn't know for sure how she was going to get inside the building, but hoped to go through the door as employees walked out. Her hooded sweatshirt covered her head, protected her baby in her belly, and hid the pistol in her pocket where it had been since she'd taken it from Mr. Todd's apartment. She worried about her baby. He, as Sheryl called the child, hadn't moved in several days, and that wasn't good. She had to keep him safe.

The door opened and several more people walked through it. Sheryl slipped in behind them, but someone bumped into her shoulder, pushing her back, and she didn't reach the entrance before the massive steel door clunked shut. It opened again and she stood face to face with Kerry Noland and a small army of fancy-dressed men. They looked bewildered, like old Red Fred when he read something in the paper he didn't understand. "We should have regular update lunches like this more often," Kerry said over her shoulder. "I'm anxious to hear how your departments are progressing." A smile, followed by tiny wrinkles, crossed Miss Noland's face. When she saw Sheryl, recognition, surprise, and fear replaced the smile.

Sheryl didn't like what she was about to do, but it was necessary — important. She backed away, staring at the evil lady. This was it. The woman needed to pay for her sins. Pulling the gun from her sweatshirt pocket, Sheryl shouted, "You're guilty. You know what you done." She pointed the gun. "You killed Mr. Todd. You ran over that man on the bike and Mr. Todd shot hisself." Bell employees scattered like rats in a gutter when a cat came along.

Seeing the gun, Miss Noland pulled up her hands and backed away. "Wait a moment... I can explain..."

"There ain't nuthin' to 'splain. I saw you do it. I saw you leave."

"But things are different, now."

Some people came back and a crowd formed a semi-circle around the pair. Several of the people who had just walked through the office doors joined the group.

"You should be punished," Sheryl said. She had never shot a gun before, but she had seen them on her TV at home, back when she had one, back when she had a home.

"Let's talk about this," Miss Noland said. "Come inside where we can talk privately. I'm sure we can..."

Sheryl backed away, the gun held before her. Then her baby kicked. The shock rippled through her belly, making her wince. She smiled... Her baby was alive... She doubled over. The kick hurt. She raised her head, and raised her gun and pointed it toward Miss Noland. The group of men who had walked through the door with Kerry were climbing over each other again to escape to safety. Everyone backed away again.

"Sheryl! No!" someone yelled. Mr. Jim from the shelter shouted as he ran toward her. The steel door behind Miss Noland flew open and several men in uniforms, like police, ran toward her. Mr. Jim had almost reached her when the baby kicked again. Sheryl fell to her knees and dropped the gun. She stiffened as Mr. Jim reached out, afraid he might hurt her. But his arms were strong, protective. He hugged her tight and fell to the cement. He rolled over so his back was to the guards and yelled, "It's all right. I have her. Don't hurt her."

As company police surrounded her, Sheryl searched for the gun. A blond haired man, about Mr. Todd's age, but taller, leaned over and picked it up. Sheryl recognized him from the funeral. He turned to face Miss Kerry and pointed the gun at her.

"Steve! What are you doing?" somebody yelled.

"You *are* responsible for Todd's death," the man with the gun shouted at Miss Kerry. "Let justice roll down like waters."

"Don't do it, Steve."

The gun went off. Miss Kerry doubled over and fell to her knees. Grabbing her side, she rolled to the ground.

The company policemen grabbed the man with the gun and threw him down onto the hard sidewalk.

Sheryl's baby kicked again.

"She's pregnant," Mr. Jim shouted. "We've got to get her to the hospital."

Noises around her faded. She heard ambulance sirens in the distance. Mr. Jim still held her, protected her, comforted her... She rested.

⋅ ⋅ ⋅

Two ambulances arrived, one behind the other. Angela, who was just beginning her shift, ran to help the EMTs roll the stretchers into the ER.

She stopped in her tracks when she recognized the lady on the first gurney. "Oh, my God!" It was Kerry Noland, CEO of that company Jim used to work for. Angela had seen her at the funeral.

A quick surveillance told her the woman had been shot and was unconscious. As doctors and nurses ran to assist, Angela turned to the second stretcher and was again shocked to recognize the woman strapped to it. She had also seen her at the funeral, yelling at Ms. Noland. More attendants rushed to help take the homeless woman to the examination room.

The automatic doors had no sooner closed behind the pregnant woman than Angela turned to see a large, familiar man running toward her. "Jim, what is going on?"

"Sheryl, the homeless woman, threatened to shoot Kerry Noland at the Bell offices," he said, slowing when he reached her. "She collapsed before she could pull the trigger. She's pregnant. I don't know how far along she is."

"We'll take care of her... and Ms. Noland," she said. It all clicked. Sheryl had accused Ms. Noland of causing Todd's suicide. She took her anger to the next level and planned to shoot Noland. "So you were there? You saw it?"

Jim Bishop was staring at the doors blocking the examination rooms. "Yeah." His voice sounded far away. "Kerry's assistant called me and said Bell wanted to offer to help the homeless shelter, so I went to her office. Then Sheryl showed up and all hell broke loose."

"Who shot Ms. Noland?"

"I think it was one of the Bell employees. He was also at the funeral. The authorities arrested him."

Angela placed a hand on Jim's arm and he turned to face her.

"We'll take care of them both." She smiled. "Don't worry."

Jim nodded. "I'll just hang here for a bit to see what happens," he said, turning toward the waiting area. "I'm kinda getting used to this place... Keep me informed, okay?"

Angela nodded and hurried back to the examination rooms.

When the patients had stabilized, Angela went into the lobby to give the news to Jim.

"Miss Noland is stable. But apparently the bullet damaged both her kidneys."

"That doesn't sound good." Jim stood up.

"Turns out, she was in danger of kidney failure before she was shot. She's been in a lot of pain. I don't think she knew it at the time but she has glomerulonephritis, sometimes called nephritis."

"Really?"

"It's serious. Her blood vessels are damaged causing the kidneys to stop functioning as they should. She's suffering from acute intrinsic kidney failure. We'll put her on dialysis as soon as we can."

"Does that mean she'll need a kidney transplant?"

"Probably. But that presents another problem."

"Yes?"

"She has Type O blood. It's not the rarest blood type, but Type Os can only receive organs from other type Os. It's going to be hard to find a good match." With each word the room seemed to close in around her. "They're searching for a kidney donor. Of course, those who have money can pay people for their organs. It happens. Since she is rich, she may not have as much trouble finding one."

"But there are no guarantees."

"There never are in life." As she said it, she recalled how true that had been in her own life.

"Things are going to get tougher for her," Jim said. "This kind of thing changes you."

"It does."

Jim shifted the conversation. "What about Sheryl?"

"She's in labor now. The doctors say she's early and the baby might not survive."

"That would devastate her. She seemed so determined to take care of her baby."

Angela sighed — no more news to share.

"Thanks, Angela."

CHAPTER EIGHTEEN

"We already talked about this on the phone," Jim said.

"I know. I took the call," David said. "You still don't have to do it."

"But I can. We have the same blood type. I'm healthy. I can help her."

The two brothers sat at Jim's kitchen table. David had taken the red eye from Sacramento and called Jim at 6:00 that morning to come pick him up at the airport. Jim scrounged around the kitchen — it wasn't as well-stocked since Jean had passed — and found some eggs, bacon, and pancake mix. David ate almost everything Jim prepared.

"No way, Jim. You can't go through with this."

"Yes, I can, and I will." They had been arguing since David climbed into Jim's Escalade.

"You are undoubtedly the most stubborn man I know," David said.

"Check the mirror, Bro."

"You don't need to do this. You told me the woman is rich. She can buy a kidney from anywhere in the world."

"But I can do this. The hospital says I'm a perfect match. We have the same blood type."

"So, what? The woman fired you. She doesn't deserve it."

"I'm going to do this because I can. Jean would do it."

"I thought you told me Jean hated Kerry No-man's-land, or whatever-her-name is."

"Noland, but that's irrelevant. Jean would have been willing to donate a kidney to anyone who needed it. Even Kerry."

"Well," David said. "It's a bad idea. I vote no."

"This isn't a democracy."

"It should be."

"Look, man," Jim said, toning down the ridiculous argument. "I really appreciate your concern." And he did. It was unusual for David to show such empathy, and it was a trait Jim welcomed.

"I'm gonna put my stuff away." David had brought a small duffle bag which he carried back toward the spare bedroom. Halfway down the hall, he stopped and turned around.

"Time to clear up my debts. Here is two hundred dollars I owe you," David said.

Jim separated the bills and stacked them up — four fifty-dollar bills. "What's this all about?"

"Remember that gun you got from that friend of yours. You were trying to figure out how to get rid of it. So, I thought I'd take care of it for you."

Jim knew David had taken it. He just had never brought it up. "What did you do?"

"I didn't make it to the Sherriff's office. Up on Independence I saw this pawn shop and decided I could get rid of it there. No questions. They sell guns, after all."

David added, "So a guy in the store said he could find someone who wanted it and he gave me two hundred dollars and here you go."

Jim placed the stack of bills to one side of the table. "You never turned in the gun?"

"No, but I got you two hundred dollars."

"But it's still out there. Someone could still use it..."

David turned back down the hall. "Don't worry about it."

"And you call me stubborn," Jim mumbled. Still, he was glad his kid brother showed interest, initiative and concern.

Five minutes later there was a knock on the front door and Jim opened it to Rev. Allen Rhodes, who said, "I heard a rumor..."

"Angela!"

"Enough said," Allen, hands up in a surrender pose said, backing down. "What you're doing is a noble gesture..."

"It's necessary, but it's not just a gesture. I wanna help."

Jim poured two cups of coffee and the friends sat at the kitchen table, where Jim and his brother had sat just moments before, where he used to sit with Jean every morning, a long time, but really, only a few months, ago.

"You know I'll be praying for you," Allen said.

"Yeah." He welcomed Allen's prayer.

"Have you heard anything about the man who shot her?" Allen asked.

"He used to work with Todd. Had become a friend, of sorts. I guess he believed Sheryl and took matters into his own hands."

"She may very well have been right."

The two men sat in silence for a long time.

"I want you to know we're going to take the Greensboro church," Allen said.

"I thought so."

"It'll be a good move for Paul."

Jim nodded. "When do you leave?" he asked.

"Not 'til June. Grace and Paul have already moved. We rented an apartment. She put him in a school there where he'll be able to have a fresh start."

"Do you think that's enough?"

"No, but it's a beginning. We've also arranged counseling... for Paul and for us."

"Good move." He reached over to the side of the table and took the stack of money. Handing it to Allen, he said, "On your first Sunday at your new church, put this in the offering plate."

Allen took the cash. "What's this?"

"Nothing. Drop it in the plate."

"Thanks," Allen said.

Before putting the bills in his pocket, Jim noticed a row of scabs on Allen's knuckles. He reached across the table and held his wrist. "What happened?"

"Nothing, really. I was fixing some pipes at home and the wrench slipped. I scraped my knuckles on the side of the cabinet." He examined the wound.

"You should have a doctor take a look at that."

"It'll be fine. These things heal up pretty quickly."

Jim let go of his hand, stared out the bay window, and thought about Allen's recent trials. "I'll miss you, my friend."

Allen had to go back to the office so he said a prayer, longer than usual, and let himself out the front door.

Jim stayed by the bay window. He sipped his coffee. The cup trembled in his hand.

The night before her kidney transplant operation, Kerry lay in a hospital room surrounded by flowers and Get Well cards but empty of friends as thoughts and fears swirled about in her head. A tray of the hospital's finest food sat before her untouched. She just wanted to fall asleep but couldn't quiet the voices in her head.

The door to her room opened and she raised her head as Jim Bishop walked in. Someone had told her he was the donor, but no one knew why. His presence surprised and embarrassed her. He pulled up a chair next to her bed, examined her tray full of food, squinted his nose, and took it away, placing it on a nearby counter. Then he reached into one pocket of his overcoat, withdrew a fast food hamburger, and placed it on the sliding table before her. He took a can of soda from his other pocket, poured some of it into a plastic cup, and set that on the table, as well. He turned back to her hospital food tray and took a knife from the little plastic bag of sterile silverware, and sliced the hamburger in two. Holding his half-can of soda in the air he said, "A toast: To a future full of thousands of tomorrows."

Kerry raised her plastic cup, touched it to his soda can, and took a sip. Then she tasted the slab of greasy meet wrapped in a white sesame seed bun and laid back against her pillow to savor its flavor. "That is so much better than hospital food."

Jim smiled. "I think it's even better than that five-star restaurant in Chicago." Jim reached back to her tray and took a little packet of salt. Tearing it open he tapped it, spilling tiny grains onto the other half of hamburger. He reseated the top of the bun and took a bite. "Much better."

She chuckled. "You know too much of that stuff will kill you," she said.

"We all gotta go sometime."

She took the salt packet from him and dribbled it onto her sandwich. After a bite she said, "You're right. It does taste better." Then she set the greasy sandwich down on the plastic wrapper. "Why are you doing this... donating your kidney?"

"Because I can," he said. "We're a perfect match – a zero mismatch, the doctor called it – and you need one kidney."

She laughed. "I honestly never thought of you and I having anything in common. After all, I pursued you... for the challenge."

"That's far behind us, now."

"Jim, I'm sorry... for everything," she said.

He reached out and took her hand in his.

"Maybe... But it must have affected you... your life."

He nodded. "Decisions have consequences."

"Yes, they do."

"What's next, when you get out of here?" Jim asked. He sat back in his chair.

She was feeling better than when he first entered her room. "I'm gonna eat more fast food... with salt," she said.

"Good idea. Better get that approved from the Doc."

She pushed her tray back a bit, relaxed into her elevated bed and said, "I wish I had a chance to treat the employees of Bell better, but instead I'll probably go to prison. The word is going around that I hit the biker and that I covered it up. It's only a matter of time."

Jim nodded. He knew. "Maybe the judge will be lenient.

She asked, "What's next for you... after the operation?"

"I'm thinking about volunteering at a suicide hotline organization. I know a little about phone service." He winked. "Thanks to a boss who required all employees to take company training in telephone customer service."

She squeezed the ridge between her eyes with her thumb and forefinger. "That's noble."

"No, it's necessary."

She felt her shoulders slump. Her eyes threatened to close. Her illness and the meds and the stress of the pending operation were dragging her down.

Jim rose. "You need to get some rest. Tomorrow is a big day and you're going to need your strength."

She nodded.

"Thanks for having dinner with me," he said with a wink and a smile. He turned and left the room, and she fell asleep and dreamed a nice dream about her father, as she had every night since her return to Charlotte.

CHAPTER NINETEEN

Angela could not recall seeing a lovelier sight. Royal purple banners hung in front. Bouquets of lilies, daisies, and violets filled a large basket between the two and on tables throughout the hall. Brilliant light streamed through every window. She held hands with Emma in the back of the chapel, taking in the beauty of the adornments.

"How have you been?" Reverend Allen Rhodes asked as he greeted her from a side door. "Is this your daughter?" he asked, bowing just a bit to greet her.

"This is Emma," Angela said, "and we're doing all right." She and her daughter both wore green and white dresses, perfect for the beginning of spring.

Doctor Jeremy Lichtner entered through the front door and Emma ran to greet him with an enthusiastic hug. "There's my date," Angela smiled. "Actually, we've only gotten together a couple of times, but Emma seems to like him a lot."

"That is so important. She looks happy. So does he."

"Yes, they both do," Angela beamed. "I don't know if you heard, but Emma, had some struggles... issues with her father. Jeremy helped me find a counselor for her. Emma likes her and I think they'll get along well."

"I'm glad to hear that. Springtime is such a wonderful time to start anew."

"I feel so very fortunate. Some girls face much worse situations than Emma did."

Allen tilted his head and his right eyebrow rose. Her comment seemed to have confused him.

"Her father seems to have changed a lot in the last week or so. He used to demand weekly visitations with Emma and coached her travel softball team, but he cancelled them. He says it's time for him to move on and only expects to see her on her birthday and at Christmas. That's a big change. I guess my attorney was quite persuasive."

Allen smiled.

"This is so beautiful," Angela said, turning back to the ornate sanctuary.

"The flowers came from Sunday's Easter service. I think it's fitting, don't you?"

She nodded, still taking in the beautiful decorations.

"We're going through some changes, too... starting anew. We're moving to Greensboro in a couple of months. I'll be pastoring a church there in June."

"I hope it's a good opportunity for you."

"I think it will be. I'm looking forward to it."

There was an awkward pause and then Angela said, "I miss him already."

"So do I. So do a lot of people," Allen said. "He was an amazing man."

Ushers opened the front doors and people filed in and moved to the front to pay respects to Jim Bishop, lying in the open casket. Angela recognized many of them.

Jim's brother, David, had flown in from California and now sat on the second row. He sat up straight, dressed in a dark suit, white shirt, and conservative tie. Several people Angela assumed were neighbors, also came to pay their respects. One lady sat in an aisle seat, a service dog on the carpet beside her.

Kerry Noland, dressed in a striking dark blue suit, arrived in a wheelchair. Several men and women dressed in business attire found seats around her.

Others came through the doors wearing more humble clothes. A bald man with a huge belly seemed to lead the entourage to rows near the front. He was followed by a younger man obviously enjoying the rhythm of music playing in his earbuds. When they sat down, the first man leaned over, pulled out one earbud, and whispered something to the man who removed the devices. Several others, all races, all ages, joined them in their pews. A big man with striking red hair, carrying a thick Bible and a dignified expression, joined the crowd. A thin old man with a scraggly gray beard and a military tattoo on his arm was the next person in the group of homeless.

Then Sheryl Williams entered the sanctuary, carrying a tiny baby wrapped in a bright blue blanket and accompanied by a pediatric nurse. She spent the most time at the casket, whispering to Jim, talking to her baby, and then holding her baby up so he could view the man in the casket. She took a seat as close to the front as she could.

Angela, Emma and Doctor Lichtner moved to the pew behind Sheryl and cooed to the beautiful baby boy.

Reverend Rhodes welcomed everyone, saying the church was fortunate to have such a wonderful throng of worshipers. He gave a powerful, moving elegy, celebrating the life of a man who took an opportunity to make a difference in his world.

After the service most of the people moved down the road to a cemetery where Jim Bishop was laid to rest next to his wife, Jean. Allen joined Angela, Emma, and Jeremy after the grave-side service. Angela said, "Knowing an exceptional man like Jim changes things. It makes you want to be better — to live a better life."

Allen nodded.

Angela glanced over her shoulder and saw Sheryl with her baby standing by Jim's grave.

⁕

Never, in her wildest dreams, would Sheryl have imagined a gift as nice as this. The apartment had a bedroom, a kitchen, and a living room — with a couch and a small TV! The refrigerator was full of food — more than she had seen in a long time. She hadn't slept in a bed like that in... at least three years.

She carried her baby from one room to the next and back again, over and over, staring at all the wonderful things. They had a lamp! And a small dining table with four chairs! And a bedside table with another lamp! And a crib and a rocking chair, like the one she had when Danielle was born where she'd rocked her to sleep every night. And kitchen stuff, like pans and silverware and glasses.

Down the hall, outside her apartment was a break room that could be shared by all the residents. "Home," she whispered. The word sounded so nice. It had been a long, long time.

Less than a month earlier they took her to the hospital after that evil woman was shot. She had her baby there — they called him a preemie, but she called him a miracle. The first time she held him in her arms — lying in that hospital bed — and stared into his bright blue eyes, she called him, Jimmy. Didn't have no middle name. Didn't need one. Jimmy Williams was fine.

One of the nurses — a black lady named Trinity — told Sheryl she had an angel watching over her. She said people didn't get second chances this good and that she should thank her lucky stars. Sheryl didn't think lucky stars existed. If they did, they were for TV and cereal boxes and rich people. People like her — they didn't have lucky stars. But she was lucky. Very lucky.

The evil lady wasn't so bad after all. She told the police she didn't want to put Sheryl in jail. Then, when she got out of the hospital, she arranged for her to stay in a motel. She had to leave Jimmy in the hospital for a few more days — they said he was too young to go with her. She knew he would be safe there, but still went to the hospital every day to see him.

They brought the two of them to this place Miss Kerry's company had set up for her. She and Jimmy were the first "guests" and more families would come soon. The tiny complex housed six apartments. Miss Kerry's company had also added a nursery for people who worked there and soon she would be able to leave Jimmy in the nursery for a few hours each day, although she didn't think she wanted to leave him anywhere.

Someone from Miss Kerry's company said she could get a job there later. She'd probably start out as a cleaning person, or in the new company cafeteria. Then, if she did well, they said she might be able to learn how to use their fancy machines and the telephones. It would be hard, but it was a start. And she was determined to succeed for Jimmy.

Things had certainly changed. She looked into the child's eyes and remembered where it all began. It was that night in the shelter when she met Mr. Jim, a tall, broad-shouldered man who also had bright blue eyes. He had been friendly. He tried to talk with her, but she didn't feel like talking. A few days later he tried to get her to go to a clinic to help with her baby, but she didn't wanna go. She saw Mr. Jim a few more times at the shelter and he always was real friendly... but not too pushy. She liked that.

Then the day Miss Kerry got shot and all those security people were running toward her, Mr. Jim got to her first and wrapped his big arms around her and kept her from being hurt. Right after that, her baby wanted to come out, so they took her from Jim and put her in an ambulance and then to the hospital where Jimmy was born.

She was real sad to hear Mr. Jim was in a coma for three days and then sadder to learn that he'd died, but they said he did it to help Miss Kerry. Sheryl thought of him looking down on her and baby Jimmy and smiling real big — like he did when he saw her in the shelter.

Somehow, Sheryl knew little Jimmy would have a smile like that. He'd be a happy boy with friends and warmth and love. She would make sure of that.

OTHER BOOKS BY BEN SHARPTON

The 3rd Option

2nd Sight

Camp Fear

ABOUT THE AUTHOR

Everyone loves a good story. Ben Sharpton has been telling them all his life to illustrate, motivate and entertain.

In 2019, he received an MFA degree (his third master's degree) from Queens University in Charlotte, in Creative Writing. *The Awakening of Jim Bishop: This Changes Things* follows four award-winning thrillers set in the South. Sharpton has also written nonfiction books, corporate, nonprofit and college curriculum, magazine articles and short stories. He currently lives outside beautiful Asheville, NC.

NOTE FROM THE AUTHOR

Word-of-mouth is crucial for any author to succeed. If you enjoyed *The Awakening of Jim Bishop*, please leave a review online—anywhere you are able. Even if it's just a sentence or two. It would make all the difference and would be very much appreciated.

Thanks!
Ben Sharpton

We hope you enjoyed reading this title from:

BLACK ROSE
writing™

www.blackrosewriting.com

Subscribe to our mailing list – *The Rosevine* – and receive **FREE** books, daily deals, and stay current with news about upcoming releases and our hottest authors.
Scan the QR code below to sign up.

Already a subscriber? Please accept a sincere thank you for being a fan of Black Rose Writing authors.

View other Black Rose Writing titles at
www.blackrosewriting.com/books and use promo code
PRINT to receive a **20% discount** when purchasing.

CPSIA information can be obtained
at www.ICGtesting.com
Printed in the USA
LVHW040616230122
709144LV00007B/719